The Hilltop Boys on Lost Island

Cyril Burleigh

Esprios.com

The HILL TOP BOYS on LOST ISLAND

Cyril Burleigh

THE HILLTOP BOYS

ON LOST ISLAND

BY

CYRIL BURLEIGH

AUTHOR OF "THE HILLTOP BOYS" AND OTHER STORIES

1917

He plunged the blade into the creature's vitals

CONTENTS

I	THE FLOATING ACADEMY
II	JACK'S DARING RESCUE
III	THE UNEXPECTED HAPPENS
IV	CAUGHT ON LOST ISLAND
V	EXPLORING THE ISLAND
VI	A WALK UNDER WATER
VII	A REMARKABLE FIND
VIII	DISCUSSING THE FIND
IX	THE LAST VISIT TO THE WRECK
X	A THRILLING ENCOUNTER
XI	THE VOICES IN THE WOODS
XII	ADVENTURES IN THE WOODS
XIII	A STRANGE LIGHT AT SEA
XIV	THE MAN WITH THE WHITE MUSTACHE
XV	JESSE W. IS SENT FOR HELP
XVI	BEN'S STRANGE STORY
XVII	DISCOVERIES AND DISAPPOINTMENTS
XVIII	IN THE LAIR OF THE FOX
XIX	THE WAY OUT FOUND

CHAPTER I

THE FLOATING ACADEMY

"Well, if this is a life on the ocean wave or anything like it, I am satisfied to remain on shore."

"I knew that the Hudson river could cut up pretty lively at times, but the frolics of the Hudson are not a patch on this."

"They said we would not be seasick, but if I am not I don't know what you call it. I don't want it any worse, at any rate."

"They said it wouldn't hurt any if you were sick, but I wonder if they ever tried it themselves?"

"No, they are like the old bachelors who write about how to bring up children. They never had any, so they don't know anything about them."

"Well, if we get much more of this I shall get out and walk."

"And I'll go with you, my boy."

There were three boys on the deck of a large steam yacht, now about two days out from New York, bound to the West Indies on a voyage combining pleasure and education.

The boys belonged to the Hilltop Academy, situated in the Highlands of the Hudson, and their names were Billy Manners, Harry Dickson, and Arthur Warren, all being close chums, and ready to share any adventure except that of being seasick.

They were none of them sick, but they were all afraid they would be, hence their remarks upon the subject.

There were close upon a hundred of the Hilltop Boys, and they were now on a tour of the islands of the Spanish Main, having been invited by the father of one of them, a man largely interested in the shipping business, who had put at their service a commodious steam yacht large enough to hold them all.

Besides the boys there were Dr. Theophilus Wise, the principal, and a number of his instructors, the negro coachman at the Academy, who was now serving in the capacity of cook and general handy man to the doctor and the boys, and the captain and crew, a considerable party all told.

The sky was bright, there was none too much motion, and there was really no reason why a lot of healthy boys should be seasick, and perhaps they only feared they would be, and were just a little uncomfortable.

They were to spend the Easter vacation and a few weeks longer among the islands, continuing their studies as usual, and getting a knowledge of geography and of many other things, which they could not get by merely studying books, Dr. Wise having practical ideas on these points, and having now a chance to carry them out through the generosity of Mr. Smith, the shipping merchant, who had furnished the yacht.

His son, Jesse W., one of the youngest boys at the Academy, had been found and brought home when lost on the mountains by one of the Hilltop boys by the name of Jack Sheldon, a general favorite at the Academy, and it was in recognition of this act that he had decided to give the boys this glorious vacation.

As the three boys were complaining about the rough seas, and the chance of becoming seasick, they were joined by two others, one of whom said in a breezy voice and with a lively air:

"Well, boys, how are you enjoying yourselves? Glorious weather, isn't it? Fine breeze, just the thing to send us along, although we do not need it, going under steam."

"I'm glad you like it, Jack!" said Harry with a wry face, "but I can't say that I do. You may be used to the water, but I am not."

"I have never been at sea before," laughed Jack, "so I cannot be any more used to it than you are. Perhaps you have been eating too much, that might make you sick. You don't look it, at any rate."

"I don't know how I look," muttered Billy Manners, stopping suddenly in his walking, "but I know how I feel," and he made a dash for the cabin, and was gone for some time, the others continuing their walk on deck.

In a few minutes a smiling negro in a white jacket and cap came out of the cabin carrying a tray containing cups of beef tea, which he offered to the boys, saying with a grin:

"Dis ain't like de beef soup yo' get at de 'cademy, sah, but mebby yo' would like a bite or two dis mon'in' to sha'pen yo' appetite fo' dinnah?"

"No, thanks, Bucephalus," said one of the boys, Dick Percival by name, who was walking arm in arm with Jack. "I don't need anything to sharpen my appetite, which is always good on sea or land."

"The idea of offering a fellow anything to eat when he feels as I do," growled Harry. "Take it away, Buck, or I'll throw you overboard."

The high sounding name of the negro was often contracted to Buck by the Hilltop boys, as in the present instance, but he was used to both, and answered as readily to one as to the other, now saying with a broad grin:

"Dat am a mistake, Mistah Harry. De worser yo' feel, de mo' yo' should put in yo' stomach, dat is to say when yo' get good nourishmental food like dis yer. Of co'se dey is detrimental substances which — —"

"That sort of talk will make me sick if nothing else will," said Harry, hurrying away, while Jack and Dick sat down, and gazed out upon the horizon, while sipping their bouillon and nibbling at their biscuits.

"We will be in summer seas, as the advertisements call them, before long," said Jack. "The air is pleasant enough as it is. Down here in the summer it is pretty hot I take it, but in April it will be all right."

"Think of us cruising around the Spanish main where the old buccaneers used to roam," laughed Dick. "Perhaps we will dig up a pot of gold buried on one of the islands by some of them."

"If Captain Kidd had buried all the gold that folks said he did," replied Jack, "he would have been kept busy till now. If people would work instead of trying to find gold that was never buried, they would accomplish something. The only treasure you dig out of the earth is the good crop you get by working at your corn and potatoes."

"That's true philosophy, Jack. I have never had to dig anything for myself, having rich folks who always looked after me. Perhaps it would have been better for me if I had had to do more for myself."

"Well, you are not a spoiled child, Dick," said Jack, "as some sons of rich parents are. You are not idle nor vicious, and you know the value of money. You will do for yourself when you leave school. You are going through a training now, that will do you good later."

"Yes, I suppose so, but your having to do for yourself has made you a stronger, more self-reliant fellow than I will ever be."

"Oh, I don't know," returned Jack, half laughing, half seriously. "I am not patting myself on the back, Dick."

"No, you never would."

The two boys were great friends, and were the leading spirits in the Academy, having a great many friends, and being looked up to by the greater part of the boys, and especially by the younger ones, who took them as models.

Dick was somewhat older than Jack, and was farther along in his classes, having had more advantages, but Jack was studious and ambitious, and bade fair to catch up with his older companion and schoolmate before many months had passed, having already in the few months he had been at the Academy greatly shortened the lead which Percival had in the beginning.

Two days later the yacht was in much pleasanter waters, and the air was quite warm and balmy, the boys going around in lighter clothing than before, wearing mostly white flannel or duck, canvas shoes and caps, and no waistcoats, some wearing only white trousers and shirts, and belts around their waists, so as to get the most comfort they could.

They were among the islands now, and expected to make a landing in a day or so, when they were farther down the Spanish main than they were at that time, the islands in the lower latitudes being more interesting in the doctor's opinion than the larger and better known ones.

It was a pleasant afternoon; none of the boys felt any touches of seasickness now, and many of them were walking up and down the deck, some taking their comfort under awnings spread aft near the cabin companion, and some being on the bridge watching the steersman or looking out to sea in search of sails or noting the flight of the gulls and other seabirds or studying the movements of the dolphins playing around the bow, there being many of these lively creatures about.

Dick and Jack were on the bridge whence they could obtain a full view of the deck and look all about them, ahead and astern, and on all sides, Jack greatly enjoying gazing out upon the wide expanse and searching the horizon for sails or a hazy view of some distant island.

Below, on the quarter deck, which was guarded by a low rail only, was young Jesse W. Smith, who took great pride in his full name and always insisted upon being called by it, for whom primarily this expedition had been gotten up, strutting up and down in sailor's trousers and shirt, seeming to feel as if he were the commander of the entire southern fleet.

"There's young Jesse, enjoying himself and seeming ready to say with the fellow in the poem that he is monarch of all he sees," laughed Dick.

"That was supposed to be Alexander Selkirk, the original Robinson Crusoe, Dick," said Jack. "The line is 'I am monarch of all I survey.' You must have recited it more than once in your younger days. That is not altogether a safe place for young Jesse W., though. That rail is not very high, and if we should happen to give a roll——"

"You don't think there is any danger, Jack! Hadn't you better warn him!"

"No, but I will go down and——" and Jack started to go to the main deck and speak quietly to the boy. But before he had hardly said the words there was a sudden startled cry and Jack, looking down quickly, saw that the very thing he had feared had taken place.

How it came about no one knew, but all of a sudden there was a loud cry of "man overboard!" and Jack saw the boy just going down in the water.

He was on the lower deck in a moment, and in another had thrown aside his coat and kicked off his shoes, running to the rail as he did so.

The cook had just been killing chickens on the forward deck, and was going aft with two or three fowls in one hand, a knife in the other.

As Jack reached the rail he saw something out on the water, just where the boy had gone down that made him turn icy cold in a moment.

Snatching the knife from the cook's hand, he sprang to the rail and leaped overboard, taking neither rope nor life preserver with him.

"By George! that's just what Jack feared, and there he is going to the rescue before any one has shouted, almost!" exclaimed Percival, as he hurried below.

"H'm! pretty clever of Sheldon," sneered a stout, unprepossessing boy, who seemed to be always scowling. "Knocks the kid overboard, and then goes to his rescue to make himself solid with the father. Very clever stroke, that, and just like him!"

"If you say anything like that of Jack Sheldon, Pete Herring," stormed Dick, who had heard the ill-natured remark, "I'll knock you overboard!"

Herring, who was by no means a favorite in the Academy, quite the reverse, in fact, had not supposed that Percival had heard his uncalled for and utterly false assertion, and now hurried away with a snarl, evidently fearing that Dick would carry out his threat.

The captain, as soon as possible, gave orders to stop the engines, and to hold the yacht near to the place where the boys had gone down, being ready to turn and go to their assistance when they should appear again.

All was excitement on board, for, until now, nothing had happened out of the ordinary, and no one thought of being seasick or of complaining of the monotony of the voyage.

Jack came to the surface, looked around him, saw young Jesse W. just coming up and shouting for help while he swam, and then, not far behind, what had caused him to take the knife with him, the sharp dorsal fin of a good-sized shark moving rapidly through the water.

CHAPTER II

JACK'S DARING RESCUE

Straight toward the swimming boy swam Jack, rapidly estimating the distance between them and the distance to be covered by the shark, the presence of which was not yet known by the younger boy.

He could swim, but he was more or less encumbered by his clothes, wide bottomed trousers and full shirt, and could not make as good progress as Jack in any event.

Then, as he was only a little fellow, and probably not accustomed to swimming very far out of his depth, Jack looked for his strength giving out at any moment.

"Keep up, J.W., you are doing fine!" he shouted, swimming straight on with a long, even stroke, which carried him rapidly toward the struggling boy.

Then some one on the yacht, with more anxiety than good judgment, shouted out so that all could hear him:

"Look out for the shark, look out!"

The instant that the younger boy heard this, he turned his head and cast a frightened look behind him, seeing the sharp fin just beginning to turn over in the water.

"Don't look, Jesse W., don't look, swim straight ahead!" cried Jack, who had come up with the boy.

Then he dove deep down so as to come up under the shark before he could turn and rush at the boy so near him.

Down went Jack, and presently began to rise, seeing the white belly of the man eater just above him.

With a fierce upward thrust of his right arm, which held the knife he had taken from the cook, he plunged the blade into the creature's vitals, drawing it downward and toward him, and turning his hand as he drew, thus making a jagged cut, and fairly laying open the shark's belly.

Young Smith, encouraged by Jack's shout, had darted ahead with his little remaining strength, not again looking back, and knowing too well what was about to happen when Jack dove.

As the shark, mortally wounded, floated away, to be eaten by others of his kind, Jesse W. suddenly became faint and felt himself giving out.

Jack arose in a moment, however, and called out cheerily:

"Hold on a moment, young fellow, and I'll be there. You mustn't give out yet, because they haven't put about to take us aboard."

The younger boy held out till Jack reached him, but seemed about to go under again when Jack said quickly:

"Here, get on my back and you won't have to swim. I'll tow you all right, and you can get rested."

"Did you kill him, Jack?" gasped the younger boy, as he obeyed the older one's instructions.

"Yes, yes, but never mind about that. Don't look behind you, just look straight ahead. I don't know that there's anything there anyhow, but it is always a good plan to look the way you're going to avoid accidents."

"You're a funny fellow, Jack," said the other. "You don't want me to see the sharks and be frightened."

"That's all right, old man, but there are no sharks at present, and if any come they will be too busy taking bites out of the other to bother me for a time. H'm! they are putting about. That's all right."

"You can carry me and swim yourself all right, Jack?" asked Jesse W. "Maybe I can swim a bit myself now."

"Never you mind about that," said Jack. "You just stay on my back till I tell you to get off," and the boy swam with a good, steady stroke

The Hilltop Boys on Lost Island

toward the approaching yacht, keeping a lookout for sharks, as he knew they would be sure to appear soon, seeming to scent blood for miles.

Without letting the younger boy know that he was on the lookout he kept a strict watch on all sides for more of the rapacious creatures, and at length discovered two making for him in different directions, one of them suddenly appearing between him and the yacht, which was rapidly approaching.

"That fellow will be frightened off or perhaps go under the vessel," he thought, "but the other one is coming on pretty fast. I hope he won't get to the yacht before me."

The people on the yacht saw the shark between them and Jack, and Dick Percival seized a gun from the captain, aimed at the creature and fired, doing no great damage, but causing the voracious monster to rush off to one side, and out of his direct course.

Sharks have other fish to guide them, and without these they are helpless, which was the case with this one, who, in his sudden change of course, got away from his pilots, and had to be hunted up by them before he could get his bearings on the boys in the water.

This created a diversion in Jack's favor, and he swam on sturdily, splashing and kicking, and making a great disturbance to frighten away the second shark, which was coming alarmingly close to him.

The yacht was coming on, however, and now they bore down toward him, slackening speed a bit, one of the sailors throwing the boy a line.

Jack caught it with one hand, as it settled over his head, and said to the boy on his back:

"Hang on, young fellow, and they'll haul us both up together. You are no sort of weight, but just hang on."

Jesse W. did as he was told, and both boys were hauled on board the yacht, Dick, Harry, Arthur, Billy Manners and half a dozen others pulling in heartily on the line.

They were drawn on board just in time, for the baffled shark made one terrific jump out of water as they reached the deck, the gangway having been opened, and banged his nose against the plankshire, falling back into the sea with a great splash.

Bucephalus was at the gangway, an axe in his hand, and as the shark gave his jump he aimed a swinging blow at the monster, but failed to hit him.

"Go back dere, yo' sassy feller," he sputtered. "Ah jus' like to get one good crack at yo' an' Ah rip yo' side open. Don' yo' perambulate dis yer way again if yo' know what am salubrious fo' yo', yo'heah?"

Bucephalus was fond of using big words, but did not always use them in the most appropriate manner, so that the boys were always kept guessing as to what he was next going to say when excited.

The boys nearest the rail seized Jack and young Smith as they came on deck, and bore them in triumph to the cabin.

"Bully for Jack Sheldon!" shouted Harry, and fifty boys gave him the heartiest kind of a cheer.

"That's some nerve he showed," declared Arthur Warren, "but then, he always did have nerve, Jack did. If he didn't he wouldn't have done the things he has."

"H'm! anybody could do that," said Herring with a snarl. "The yacht was close to him all the time. You fellows are all the time cracking up Jack Sheldon, but I don't see that he is any great shakes."

"No, you wouldn't," said Billy Manners, with an emphasis on the pronoun, "but decent fellows can see it. Would you have gone over after young Smith?"

"There wasn't any need to do it," growled Herring. "If I'd seen him first I'd have done it."

"You saw it as soon as any one except Jack himself, and you were nearer the deck," said Percival, who came up in time to hear what Herring had said. "I heard you say that Jack pushed the boy overboard so as to get the name of rescuing him. You know that this is a lie, because Jack was on the bridge at that time, and could not have done it. Jack and I both saw young Jesse W. go overboard. Jack feared he might, and had started to go to the deck when the thing happened."

Herring did not care to get into a quarrel with Percival, who was much stronger and better built than himself, and he, therefore, went away muttering something which the boys could not make out.

"He is always saying something nasty against Jack," declared Arthur. "He hates Jack because Jack is smarter, and a general favorite. I wish he had stayed on shore, but as Mr. Smith invited the whole Academy he could not very well be left behind."

"He ought to be marooned on some solitary, uninhabited island, and left there to hate himself," chuckled Billy Manners.

"They don't do those things nowadays, Billy," said Percival. "You have been reading the lives of the pirates, and are full of that sort of romantic stuff."

"Maybe I am," chuckled Billy good naturedly, "but here come Jack and young Jesse W., looking as fine as fiddles, and not a bit worse for their baths. Whoop it up for them, boys!"

Every boy in sight responded to the summons, and gave both boys the heartiest cheers, both Jack and his young companion being favorites.

CHAPTER III

THE UNEXPECTED HAPPENS

Neither Jack nor young Smith felt any the worse for his tumble into the warm waters of the Caribbean, and after they had changed their clothes they went on deck to assure their schoolmates that they were all right, and suffering no inconvenience from their trip overboard.

"Jack is a great sport," declared Jesse W., "but somebody called out 'shark!' a little too quick, for I nearly went to pieces. It may Have been kind in him, but it was injudicious, to say the least."

The boys smiled at the young fellow's wisdom, and Billy Manners replied:

"Well, it wasn't me, J.W., although I know I do a good many fool things. You can't lay that at my door, however."

"Oh, you are a facetious fellow, and keep us amused, but you do think of things," replied the younger boy. "The person who shouted 'shark,' is one of the sort who yell 'fire' at the first sign of smoke, and raise a panic in a crowded hall. They should be suppressed."

"Very true, J.W., you have the right of it," said Billy, smiling. "You get the right idea under your bonnet now and then."

Young Smith had always been fond of Jack, but he was more so now and stuck close to the older boy on all occasions, saying the next day to Jack as they were walking on deck:

"Do you know, Jack, you have done a lot for me, and it is time I did something for you. I am going to speak to my father about you. It is a bit of a job for you to get your schooling and your living and everything, isn't it?"

"Well, it is not so easy, Jesse W., and I do have a tussle now and then," returned Jack, smiling at the other boy's earnestness. "Still, one has to work for what he gets in this world."

"Unless he steals it, and there is no satisfaction in that," said the smaller boy wisely. "And later he has to work—in jail. What I wanted to say was that now you have done this last thing for me, saving my life, that's what it was, I think my father would like to do something for you, help you through your schooling or something like that. Of course you would not want him to give you money, for he does not put a commercial value on my life, but he could help you to get ahead and so help yourself, couldn't he now, Jack?"

"I suppose he could," Jack laughed, "and you are a thoughtful young fellow, J.W., but never mind about that. One of the sailors, Bucephalus, any one, in fact, could have done what I did. In fact, it is all in the day's work at sea, and nothing is thought of it."

"No, but no one else did it, Jack. Any one might, but no one did. Only you. Any one else could have done it, but they did not all the same. That's nonsense about your pitching me overboard. I heard some of them talking of it. Why, you were not there. I was on the quarter deck, where I had no business to be, I suppose, with just a little bit of a low rail, and when the vessel took a sudden roll I went overboard."

"Jack saw you up there," said Percival, who was walking with the others, "and spoke about warning you that it was dangerous. In fact, he was on the way to tell you when you got ahead of him and rolled overboard."

"Jack is all the time thinking of some one," said young Smith. "That's what makes him different from the other Hilltop boys."

"Oh, then you don't think I think of others, eh? That's one on me."

"Oh, you haven't had to, Dick, you have always had some one to think for you," said Jesse W. wisely, and both Dick and Jack laughed.

"That young fellow will be doing something for you, Jack," said Percival a few minutes later when the two happened to be alone. "He is thinking of it now, and later you will hear from it."

"I suppose he will," said Jack thoughtfully, "and I don't know how I can stop him. I could not help doing what I did, but you would have done the same if you had seen the danger before I did."

"But I did not," returned Dick, "and that is just young Smith's line of argument. It is nothing that you could have done something if you don't do it. Well, you deserve all that can be done for you, and that is all there is about it, old chap."

Two days later in the middle of the afternoon, the day having been warm with very little air stirring so that the boys were glad to seek the shelter of the awnings spread across the decks, the breeze suddenly fell away and the air became fairly stifling.

The captain looked anxious, and ordered the awnings taken down, and told the boys that they had better go below.

Dr. Wise and the professors got the boys below, and none too soon, for all of a sudden a funnel-shaped cloud appeared on the horizon, spread with startling rapidity until it covered the entire heavens, and then from it shot out a fierce flash of lightning, while the wind which had died out now blew from an unexpected quarter with the greatest fury.

Being under their own steam they, of course, had no use for sails, which would have been blown away.

For all that the waves dashed them ahead with great rapidity and the propellers were now high out of water and now buried deep in the sea, the yacht being almost unmanageable.

The wind was behind them, and there was no chance of going about in such a blow and with such great waves dashing against them, so in pitch darkness they sped on, no one knew where.

The electric lights in the cabin and the saloons were turned on so that the boys were not in darkness, and some of the officers moved about among them telling them that this was simply a squall, and would soon blow itself out, and that there was nothing to be feared.

The howling of the gale, the creaking and straining of the shrouds, the thumping and pounding and groaning of the machinery, and the tramping of men overhead made a combination of sounds that might well terrify anyone, and the older boys tried to reassure the younger ones that it would be over in a short time, and that they would soon be sailing on smooth seas again, and be laughing at their former terrors, but it took a great deal of faith to make all this believed, and some of those who urged it had very little confidence in its truth.

Herring, Merritt, and others of the same class were really terrified, and took on dreadfully, predicting all sorts of dreadful things, and declared that they were fools to have taken this voyage, and that they would never undertake another.

Jack Sheldon, Dick Percival, Harry Dickson, and even mercurial Billy Manners were quite different, however, and young Jesse W. Smith acted like a man, and although he was frightened, as any one might be, and no shame to him, did not give way to his fright, but said very wisely that he guessed the storm had been gotten up for their especial benefit so that they might know what sort of things they could do in these latitudes.

How long they were rushing before wind and sea they did not know, for it seemed ages, where they were going they could not guess either as they had come from an unexpected quarter, and so suddenly that they had not noticed its direction, and were not where they could look at the compass.

All was bright and cheerful in the cabins, but through the portholes they could see that all was dark outside with an occasional vivid flash of lightning, these coming less and less frequent at length till they ceased, and then the skies began to brighten.

Suddenly, however, before it was yet bright enough outside to make out any objects, there was a sudden rush forward as if they had been struck by a great wave, then a sudden upheaving as if they were mounting to the sky, then another long rush forward, and then a shock as if they had struck something, and for a few moments the lights went out.

When they flared up again the vessel seemed to be at anchor, and the boys said to each other:

"What is the matter, have we struck on a rock, are we sinking, what is the matter anyhow?"

There was no confusion on deck, as there would have been if what the boys feared had really happened, and presently one of the officers came below and said reassuringly:

"Well, we are all right as far as I can see, but where we are is another story. In some landlocked bay, apparently, but where it is or how we reached it I can't tell."

"We were struck by a cyclone, weren't we, Officer?" asked young Smith, with a wise air.

"That's just what it was, and when those things strike you they strike hard. Lucky for us that we happened to be going ahead of it, for if we had been head on to it we might not have survived."

"But there is no danger, we have not struck a rock or anything, we have no holes in our hull?"

"None that we can see. We are beached somewhere, and we may slide into deeper water, but as far as we can tell now we are safe enough. Where we are, however, will have to be determined when the sun comes out."

The boys were reassured by this news, and after a time some of them went out on deck, the yacht being now almost motionless, the waves just lapping their sides, and running lazily up a beach, which they could now just make out at a little distance.

It grew lighter and lighter quite rapidly, and at length the sun appeared, and they found themselves in a landlocked bay with a white beach in front of them, beyond that a thick grove of palms of various kinds, green hills on all sides and in the distance, straight ahead, a hill of considerable size crowned with a thick growth of trees.

As the sun grew brighter the scene increased in attractiveness, and the greater part of the boys were charmed by it, making many exclamations of delight, as they turned from one object to another.

"It's a fine place wherever it is," said Jack. "I suppose they will locate it to-morrow, and perhaps some one will come out to the yacht, and tell us where we are."

"I don't see any sign of dwellings," murmured Percival. "Perhaps there are no people on it. Not all of these little islands are inhabited, and I suppose it is an island?"

"Probably, for I do not think we are near the South American coast. Some one will know after a bit, doubtless. At any rate, we are safe and that is a good deal."

One of the officers came along where the two boys were standing, and Jack asked him if he knew where they were.

"No, I don't," was the answer. "We have not been able to get an observation yet, and we started off at such a gait that it was impossible to tell where we were going or at what rate. We will probably locate ourselves in the morning, but there is no danger so you can make your minds easy on that point, young gentlemen."

"There is a good deal in that, sir," said both boys.

CHAPTER IV

CAUGHT ON LOST ISLAND

The sun set gloriously, and after a short twilight common to those latitudes the full moon arose over the hills, and all the stars came out little by little till the heavens were full of them.

The moon dimmed their brightness somewhat, but they were still very brilliant, and the night was a glorious one, the air warm and balmy, the breeze just enough to temper the heat of the air, and all around them sea and shore bathed in moonlight.

After dinner, which was served in the saloon as usual, the boys went out on deck for the most part, and enjoyed the beautiful evening, being dispersed in little groups here and there, some seated and some walking the decks.

"We are safe enough, anyhow," observed Jack to Percival and a few of the boys who were seated on deck with him, "and I suppose we will not leave here till the morning at any rate."

"We are sheltered in this bay, and even if there should be a storm outside we will not feel it," returned Percival. "I hardly think there is one, and it seems strange that we should have caught that cyclone at this time of the year. Isn't it unusual?"

"You can't call anything unusual in the tropics," laughed Jack. "I believe you are liable to catch anything at any time here from yellow fever to a tornado. They seem to have them always on hand."

"Well, we are safe now, at any rate, and I am glad for that much. We will make the best of this fine night, and take other things as they come."

It was late when the last of the boys went to bed, for they all wanted to make the most of the fine night, but they were all up early the next morning, anxious to learn where they were, and if they would stay at the island or put to sea again.

Jack was the first of the boys on deck, and when he reached there he saw Dr. Wise talking to the captain and the first officer, there being a grizzled old seaman conversing with Bucephalus at a short distance.

The doctor and the officers seemed to be carrying on a very earnest conversation, and Jack heard a little of it as he came forward, and then suddenly stopped, fearing that he might be intruding.

"We are on the bottom, sir, and I don't know how long we may be there," said Captain Storms. "The next high tide may raise us, and it may not. It is my opinion that we have been on the bottom ever since we came into the bay, and how we are going to lighten her I don't know."

"But there are no holes, we have opened no seams, we have not taken in any water?" asked the doctor, looking fixedly at the captain through his big black-rimmed spectacles.

"No, there are no open seams and no water. The bottom is sandy, too, I think, and not the sharp coral rock you find in these parts that will cut a hole in anything that touches it. No, it is simply a case of too little water to float us, but that, as I may say, may be remedied. Time will tell."

"Then you do not think there is any cause for alarm, sir?"

"Not any great amount, no, sir. The moon is not quite full, although it looked so last night, and when it fills we may get higher water. We can tell to-night. Meanwhile, there are the boats, and your young gentlemen may go on shore and explore the island. I don't think there are any people on it, as it seems very small. Many of the islands hereabouts have no one on them."

"You don't know which one it is as yet?"

"No, I don't."

The doctor walked forward, and looked over the rail, and Jack went up to Bucephalus, and the old sailor and said:

"You don't know where we are, either of you, I suppose?"

"Ah haven't de remotest ideah, sah," replied the negro, "an' far as Ah can make o't dis gentleman am in de same predicament. He says we am in de tropics at a island ob not werry big size an' importance, but Ah was aware of dese fac's mahself befo' Ah interrogated him, sah, so dat Ah am no furder dan Ah was befo', sah."

"This here is an island in the Spanish Main, the place where the old pirates and buccaneers used to roam," said the old sailor whose name Jack learned later was Ben Bowline, "and that's all I know about it. You didn't come lookin' fur Cap'n Kidd's treasure, did you?"

"No, we did not, and I don't believe we would find it if we had. Men are foolish that go looking for such things. I don't believe that Captain Kidd buried the hundredth part of the gold that he is reputed to have buried. I have other things to do besides looking for buried gold."

"You're about right," said Ben, "but there's plenty who do look for it, and spend their lives at it and don't get nothing. This here is one of them islands, and I thought mebby you boys had come a-lookin' for something like that. Boys haven't anymore sense."

"Thank you, but you'll find that the Hilltop boys have a good deal more sense than that."

After breakfast two of the yacht's boats were lowered, and some of the boys went ashore to explore the island and amuse themselves in various ways while the captain sent a party to find the outlet of the bay, and see what their chances for leaving the island might be.

Jack, Percival, Harry, Arthur and young Smith went on one boat, and were the first to land, walking up the beach and into the woods as the other boat came ashore.

Picking a path as they went on Jack and his companions pushed into the deep everglade, the lush undergrowth sometimes quite impeding their progress, and making their advance very slow.

"If we were going to be here any time," said Percival, "we should have to make a path so that we could get about with greater rapidity. If we had thought to bring an axe it would have been better."

After a time their progress was more rapid, as the undergrowth was less rank, and they went on with more comfort.

Many varieties of cactus, prickly pears, plums and plants with the most gorgeous flowers lined their path, and gave constant delight to young Smith and some of the others, but Jack and Percival were more intent on seeing where they would come out than in looking at plants and flowers, and they gave the latter little attention.

"There is certainly no one on the island," said Jack at length when they came out upon an upland glade more open to the sky than the parts already traversed, "or we should have seen them by this time. I think we have been going in the same general direction, Dick, so suppose we push on in the same line, and see where we come out."

"All right, but there are hills, which we may have to climb if we keep straight on. There they are ahead of us."

"Yes, I see them, but they do not seem to be very high nor far away. If they want us back at the yacht they will probably blow the bugle."

They pushed on across the open space, and then through a wood where it was not so easy to advance and at length, without noticing it, began to descend, the way being good at times and at others very difficult so that they were frequently obliged to halt and get breath.

"I shouldn't wonder if we were the pioneers of this island," said Harry, "for no one seems to have been through here before. How do you stand it, young Smith, all right?"

"Well, it is not so easy as walking along Broadway in New York," rejoined Jesse W., "but I can manage it, I guess."

"It strikes me that we are going down instead of up," observed Arthur, "and we thought we would have to climb the hills we saw."

"You often have to go up and down two or three times in climbing a mountain," said Jack. "It looks all up from a distance, but there are often intervening valleys, which have to be crossed, and then you go up again."

"This must be a pretty deep one, then," said Harry, "for we are going down at a pretty steep incline now."

They pushed on, passing through many great masses of rock, and still going down at a decided angle until at length they came out upon a bare, rocky shore with huge masses of rock to the right and left, and beyond a line of reefs over which the surf was dashing, all being white both beyond and inside the reefs.

"We are on the other side of the island!" exclaimed Jack, "and we have not climbed our hills at all or else they were so slight that we did not notice them."

"I would not like to be in a vessel driven on this side of the island," said Percival. "See how the surf dashes over those reefs. You would go to pieces in a short time."

"That may be the reason why there are no people on it," said Jack. "It is not very big, I take it, and is probably difficult of access. We seem to have come to it without knowing it, and if we had I don't believe we would have gone near it."

They stood watching the surf, and taking in various parts of the shore, seeing a great mass of rocks higher than those at hand, to the east of the larger mass close in to land, and at length Jack suggested that they return to the other side.

"We ought to be able to follow the path we made coming across," he said, "and in any event, we know the general direction, and if we do go astray a bit it won't matter."

They set out upon their return, and came out not far from where they had started, finding Billy Manners and three or four of the boys on shore waiting for them.

"We thought you might be along soon," said Billy. "Would you believe it, they don't know what this island is after all, don't know the name of it, I mean."

"How is that?" asked Harry. "Isn't it charted?"

"Yes, it is charted all right, but there is no name given to it. The captain says it is a sort of lost island, and they never thought enough of it to give it a name or if it had one they didn't think it was good enough to put on the chart."

"Lost Island is a good enough name for us," observed Jack. "Suppose we call it that while we are here. That will not be long, I suppose."

"H'm! I don't know about that," Billy returned. "They have the yacht afloat all right. They started the engines, and backed her off a sand bank or whatever it was we were on, and are now in fairly deep water, but as to leaving the island that is another matter."

"How is it?" asked all the boys in a breath.

"Because there is a line of reefs stretching right across the mouth of the bay, and there seems to be no way of getting beyond them. There seem to be openings here and there, but they are so narrow that the captain does not think it wise to try to go through them."

"Then we are lost on Lost Island, and are lost ourselves," said Jack.

CHAPTER V

EXPLORING THE ISLAND

The boys returned to the yacht in time for dinner, and here their situation was talked over by the doctor and the captain, the former assuring the boys that there was no great danger, for the yacht was equipped with a wireless service, and the captain could easily make his predicament known, and vessels would doubtless be sent to his relief.

"We may pursue our studies as usual," the doctor continued, whereupon there were wry looks upon the faces of many of the boys, "and as soon as we get away from here we will pursue our voyage. It is simply an incident, not an accident in our plans as arranged."

After dinner Jack got one of the yacht's boats, and took Dick and young Smith with him to the mouth of the bay to get a view of the reefs.

For some little distance they could not see the opening of the bay on account of its windings, the hills preventing them from getting a view of the sea, but at length in rounding a wooded point they came in sight of it.

There were reefs in front of them, at some little distance, and points of rocks on both sides, the outer bay being of considerable size, but generally exposed to the weather, which they were not in the inner bay.

They pushed on for some little distance, but not too near the reefs, where they would be exposed to the force of the surf that dashed over the latter and Jack presently pointed out a strange looking object on his right and at some little distance.

"I should say that that was a flagstaff sticking out of the rocks," he said, "if it were not the most unlikely thing in the world that there should be one there. If any one wanted to plant a flag-pole they would go up higher on the rocks, I should think."

"See if you can get a little nearer to it, Jack," said Dick. "It looks too big for a flagstaff, but it might be the stump of a mast."

"Which is much more likely," replied Jack. "A vessel might have gone ashore there, and show the stump of a mast above water. It is a wonder to me that we were not in the same predicament."

"The only way that I account for it is that we were hit by a tidal wave or the end of one, and carried right over the reefs without scratching, and then the force of the water carried us to the inner bay where it left us stranded for a time."

"That sounds reasonable, and in the absence of any other explanation may as well be received as the right one. I think you are correct about its being the stump of a mast, Dick."

Jack rowed as close to the point of rocks as he dared, not caring to be dashed upon them, the landing being bad, and the boys got a better view of the object that Jack had noticed.

It was out in the water, and projected about five feet, and, being broken off apparently about half way to the crosstrees, should be at least that distance under water.

"I should say there was five or six feet of water there," said Jack, "and you can see from the marks on it that this broken end is still below high water mark. I don't see any sign of a bowsprit but maybe that was broken off when she struck."

"And we can't tell whether this is the fore, main or mizzen," observed Dick; "or whether she had more than two masts. There must be some of her hull left, but it is all under water and maybe deeper than you think."

"Yes," said Jack musingly, "and I am very glad that we are above it and safe, even if we are on a lost island. The tide is coming in steadily now, and there will be more surf, so I think it just as well not to be too near the reefs."

"We might get ashore at some other point farther back, and examine this part of the coast," suggested Percival.

"That woody point which we rounded and so came in sight of the outer bay might be a good place," added young Smith, who seemed a boy of ideas, although he was a little fellow and younger than the others. "We could go ashore there, I think, Jack."

"Yes, so we might," said Jack, as he began to row back. "There is time now, I think. We have not got to go right back."

He pulled on till he reached the point of woods and then looked for a good place to land, finally finding one where there was a narrow white beach and a bank which sloped gradually up to a distance of twenty feet to a ledge whence there was another rise of about twenty feet to another grassy bank.

"This seems to be a good place," he said, as he pulled in to the little beach. "Here is an old stump to which we can tie the boat so that it may not drift away from us when the tide comes in if it reaches this point."

Making the boat fast with plenty of slack to the rope in case the tide should rise high, he got out and then he and Percival ascended the first slope, helping Jesse W. between them.

There was room enough for all of them on the bank, but it did not appear to extend very far, and after taking a rest of a few minutes they set out to ascend to the next landing place where they again rested.

Here there was more room than before, but it was farther to the next stopping place, and there was still more room when that would be reached.

From this point they could see much of the inner bay, and make out the yacht at anchor, but could not see much beyond that, and Jack suggested that they go to a still higher point, and get another observation.

There were trees, big and little, and rough rocks here and there, which would aid them in making the ascent, and they kept on till they reached another good stopping place of greater extent whence they could see much more than before.

Jack and Dick helped young Jesse W. up the bank, as, otherwise, it would have been hard for the little fellow, who was under the average size for boys of his age, and he felt quite proud of being with the older boys, and said as he looked around on the water and the island and the yacht lying at anchor:

"When I tell the other fellows that I came up here they won't believe me. I tell you, it is something to have two such big fellows to look after a little shrimp like me."

"Never mind, J.W., you will grow if you will only wait," laughed Jack. "We were all little fellows once."

"What sort of place is this, anyhow?" asked the smaller boy, looking about him. "There are woods and rocks, and down there I can see that stump of a mast. I wonder if we could see more of her by——"

He was walking on, looking at the mast sticking out of water more than at the ground at his feet when suddenly Jack noticed that he was right on the edge of a hole just discernible in the tall grass.

He darted forward, and caught the boy's arm just as he was about to step into this hole without seeing it, and pulled him back.

"Look out, Jesse W., or you'll go in!" he cried. "You don't know how deep that place is nor where it will land you."

"H'm! I never noticed it. It does seem deep, doesn't it? I wonder how far down it goes, and what's at the end? Water, do you suppose?"

"I don't know, I'm sure," said Jack, "but you might have had a bad fall, my boy. You don't want to go star-gazing like that in strange places. You never know what may be in the way. Always look where you are going."

"Yes, that's good advice, but I wonder if there is anything down there anyhow? Do you suppose we could get down?"

"Possibly," returned Jack thoughtfully, "but I imagine it is a pretty good job to get down there and a bigger one to get back, and nothing down there anyhow."

"You can't tell without going down," said the younger boy wisely, as he knelt on the edge of the hole, and looked down. "Have you got a pocket light with you? We might tell something with that."

Jack parted the tall grass, and just then the sun shone out brightly, as the breeze blew aside the branches, and a broad track of sunlight was let into the hole.

"It does not go straight down," said Dick, who was now at Jack's side. "In fact, I don't think it is as steep as the path we came up. We might go down and investigate."

"Yes, but what would there be there when we got down?" asked the other half impatiently. "We ran the risk of breaking a leg or an arm just for the sake of exploring a hole in the ground, and get nothing out of it. If there was anything there, now — —"

"Yon don't know till you look, as Jesse W. just remarked, and there might be something there after all. Some of Captain Kidd's treasure, for instance."

"Nonsense! You are full of Captain Kidd's treasure, and so are half the boys. You won't find anything down there, and you will have your trouble for your pains."

"I'm going to look just for the fun of it, anyhow," said Dick, "although it would be very convenient to have a light as J.W. suggests. Another time we can bring one."

The sun shone more strongly into the hole, and Dick began to descend, using a stout stick, which he had broken from a tree near at hand, to assist him in going down.

The smaller boy looked rather wistfully into the hole as Dick went down, and Jack, breaking another stout stick, asked:

"Do you want to go down there, young fellow, and follow Dick Percival on a fool's errand?"

"It might not be that," said the other, "and I would like to go."

The Hilltop Boys on Lost Island

"All right, then, come along. Here is a staff for you. I can do without one, I think. Keep close to me. Can you walk upright, Dick?"

"Yes, generally," came back the answer in a muffled voice. "My! but the place is filled with echoes, Jack. It goes down quite a distance I should say. The light is a big help. Funny, but there seems to be a light down here, although where it comes from I can't say."

The boys kept going down and at length Jack said, pausing and trying to pierce the darkness, the light that Percival had spoken of not being visible at that moment:

"I think we would better get a light, Dick. We don't know where we are going, and it is dark. It is never safe to go anywhere in the dark unless one is familiar with his surroundings."

"That's true enough, Jack. Have you any matches? The next time we come this way, if we do, we had better take a flashlight along."

"I have matches," said Jack, and in a moment a tiny blaze shot up, increasing till it enabled them to see to some extent where they were.

They were still descending, but in a short time were on more level ground or rock, whatever it was, proceeding till the match went out, and a few steps farther when Dick suddenly brought up against something and exclaimed in surprise:

"Hello! we cannot go any farther, Jack. Strike another match, and let us see where we are."

Jack lighted two or three matches at once, and held them just above his head so as to obtain a good view of his surroundings.

"Hello! what is this?" exclaimed Percival. "A cave, or what?"

Just before them was a jagged opening into some region beyond, but whether it was a cave or not puzzled them.

Jack went closer, and held his light in the jagged opening.

"It's a hole in the side of a vessel, Dick!" he cried in amazement.

CHAPTER VI

A WALK UNDER WATER

"That's what it is, Jack," said Dick, after the first sensation of astonishment had passed. "It is more in the bow than on the side, however. You can see how she narrows a little farther on. This hole is pretty well forward. I tell you what! This is the vessel we saw under water, or the one that stump of a mast belongs to, at any rate."

"I believe it is, Dick. Probably she drove in here, had a hole smashed in her bow, and then sank. The earth has settled in between the masses of rock above and around her, and hidden her, but there is still the fissure down which we have just come."

"This is as good as finding Captain Kidd's treasure, isn't it?" exclaimed young Smith. "We never expected to find anything. Shall we go in and see what more there is, Jack?"

"We may find ourselves in the water before we know it," murmured Jack. "No, I think we would better stay where we are. It is the safest plan by long odds. It looks like taking too many chances to go into a place like that. Better wait till another time."

"Give me a match or two, Jack," said Percival. "I'll promise not to take too great a risk."

Jack handed him the matches, and he struck them, and advanced a step or two into the opening.

"It is plenty wide enough," Percival said. "Yes, these are ship's timbers, all right. She must have struck hard to make such a gash. We are on a level with the lower deck. I can't see much cargo around, but there is a way aft. This must be a sort of steerage, and the lower hold where the cargo is stored is below us. I believe we could walk right ahead to the after bulkhead, and if there happens to be a door in it, as is often the case, straight into the after cabin."

"If there were anything to make a torch of, Dick, I'd go with you," said Jack, "for I am as much interested as you are in this strange find, but we don't know what we might stumble against or into what hole we might fall. Wait, Dick. We shall not probably leave the island for some time, and there will be opportunities to find out more about it."

"Yes, I suppose so, but I would like to find them out now. However, you have the right of it, and it is just as well to be cautious."

"Besides, I have only a few more matches left, and we must get back to where we started. If you and I were alone — —"

"Yes, quite right," and Dick came out, as his matches were extinguished, and they started back.

A match or two gave them all the light they wanted till they began to ascend, the way up being more difficult than coming down, and both older boys being obliged to assist the younger one.

However, they reached the top at last, the light seeming to be almost dazzling after they had been used to the darkness for even the short time they were down in the strange place.

"I never knew the sun to be so bright," said Jesse W. "It's like what men say coming up out of a deep well is."

"We'll go there again," said Percival. "I want to know more about the place. Better not say anything to the other fellows. We'll have them swarming over the place if we do, and then there is more or less danger in going down there."

"I believe you want to keep the discovery all to yourself in case we did find treasure there," said Jack. "Probably there is nothing more than a lot of spoiled beef and some old clothes."

"Oh, after we have seen all there is to be seen I don't care, but I do want to have it to ourselves until we have had a chance to see all there is to be seen. Think of going into a vessel through a hole in the side. Very few people can say they have done that."

"There'll be no getting the vessel out of that now," said young Smith. "I wonder how old it is!"

"It cannot be so very old," replied Jack. "If she were, the moss and slime on that stump of a mast would be thicker, and there would not be so much of the stump. Probably she is filled with water in any event."

"There was none in the part we saw."

"No, as that was above water, but the lower part undoubtedly is. I do not believe we could go all the way through as Dick suggests."

They went back to the place where they had left the boat, made their way down and rowed back to the yacht, where they went on board, and saw some of the boys, telling them of visiting the reefs, but saying nothing of the strange discovery of the vessel among the rocks.

There was a very high tide that night, but Captain Storms decided that it would be very unwise to try to pass beyond the reefs, none of the openings being wide enough and the surf very heavy.

"There is no use, young gentlemen," he said to Jack and Dick and a few others. "We will have to stay here for a time until I can get in connection with the outside world. Then, perhaps, some one may know about this place, and a way out of it. One vessel has gone down here, and I don't care to be the next, and leave my mainmast sticking up out of the water to show folks the way to destruction."

"We saw that stump ourselves," said Jack. "Was that wreck long ago, do you think?"

"Not so many years, twenty, perhaps, or maybe less. The rocks would hold her tight, but I don't believe there's much left of her. Nothing worth taking away, I guess."

Jack gave Dick a peculiar look, and neither of the boys told what they had seen.

The boys had lessons and a lecture that afternoon, and again the next morning and in the afternoon were free to go about as they pleased, explore the island or go out on the water with some of the sailors.

"I want to take another look at that old vessel," said Percival to Jack after dinner. "I have borrowed a stout rope and an axe, and I have my pocket light with me. Will you go along, Jack? I suppose we should take J.W. with us, but he is a little fellow, and there might be danger."

"If we find anything whatever we can take him another time," said Jack. "I don't want anything to happen to the young fellow. Some of the boys may be saying that I took him to a dangerous place just to have the name of rescuing him again."

"You don't mind what such fellows as Herring and some of the rest say, I hope?" sputtered Percival.

"Not altogether, but it is annoying all the same."

"What those fellows need is a good thrashing."

"Well, I don't like this constant wrangling, and I keep away from them as much as possible and don't give any cause for talk."

"Which is the cheapest kind of goods dealt in. Never mind them, but come along and make another investigation of the wreck. I believe we may find something in it."

"Spoiled beef and rotten clothes," laughed Jack. "However, I will go with you, Dick."

They took the boat and rowed to the woody point where they made fast, and climbed to the top as before, having much less trouble on account of not having the younger boy to assist.

They made their rope fast to a tree near the edge of the hole among the rocks, and by its help descended to the bottom, then lighting their way to the hole in the side of the vessel.

With the axe Percival cut away the jagged edges of the timbers at the opening, and then he and Jack pushed forward, using the axe now and again as rubbish of various kinds came in their way.

They could see boxes and bales and casks on either side as they went on, there being a passage-way between the tiers of the cargo, and here and there a post or stanchion had half fallen and impeded their progress, obliging them to cut it.

As Percival had predicted, there was a door at the end of the bulkhead, dividing the hold from the cabin, but this was fast.

"It is not very thick," said Percival. "I believe I can break it in with a blow of the axe."

"Wait a moment, Dick," said Jack cautiously. "Listen! It strikes me I hear the sound of water. We don't want to let a flood in on us. It is likely that the after hold and cabin are full of water, and we don't want to be swamped."

Percival put his ear to the door, and then flashed his light through the keyhole.

"There's nothing there, Jack," he said. "If there were water it would come through here. We have gone so far, and I'd like to go the rest of the way and get to the cabin. I believe we can. There is probably a passage on one side of the companion leading to the after cabin."

"Yes, and the companion is open, and the place full of water."

"There is none here, at any rate, and it will be time enough to look for trouble when it comes," returned Percival impatiently. "Stand aside, old man, and throw the light on the door so that I can give a good blow."

Jack did as requested, and Percival raised the axe and dealt the door a sturdy blow, which took it off its hinges and sent it crashing into a narrow passage beyond.

"There is no water there!" he exclaimed in triumph. "Come on, Jack."

The two boys went into the passage, stepping over the fallen door, Jack showing the way with the pocket electric light, which was great use to them in the strange place.

The passage was narrow, not wide enough for the two boys to walk side by side, and was about two fathoms in length, leading to another door which was fast like the first.

In many vessels there is a passage like this leading from the after cabin to the steerage, where the entire hold is not open from the hatches to the keel, as in big ships, which the captain may use in reaching certain portions of the cargo with less trouble than in the case of its being stored in a solid bulk.

"Here is another door, Jack," said Percival. "I don't see any sign of a companionway from the deck."

"No," said Jack, putting his ear to the door and listening intently. "I can hear the swash of water just the same, Dick. We had better be a bit careful."

"We would hear it here, anyhow, Jack. There is water outside, and I don't suppose there is much depth here. You would be very likely to hear it the same as you hear water dashing against the side of a vessel when you are in the hold. It doesn't follow that the water is beyond there."

"No, I guess not. Well, give it a smash, and be ready to run in case there is water there."

Percival took as much room as he could in the narrow passage, swung the axe, and sent the door crashing into the space beyond.

Instead of a flood of water breaking in upon the boys, as Jack more than half expected, there was considerably more light while the sound of water was more distinguishable than before.

"Well! I declare!" exclaimed Percival, pressing forward.

The boys found themselves in the after cabin of a vessel, which was as dry as if she had been in her dock, a soft light from overhead showing them the details of the place perfectly, even without the light of the torch.

"We are under water, Jack!" cried Percival.

"So it seems."

"That light comes from the bull's-eye overhead. The water over it softens the light. Otherwise, the sun would pour right into the place."

"That would be better than having the water pouring in on us, Dick. The flashings of that skylight are tighter than most of them, however, or the water would have gotten in here long before now."

"It is just possible that the glass has been covered with sand which has been lately washed away. That would fill all the cracks around the flashings and make them tight. Very likely the wave that sent us in here has uncovered the skylight, and that is how it is light in here. It is dry, too, Jack. Why, this is like being in one of the submarines we have read of."

"Where you slide back a panel and look at the fishes in procession, through a plate-glass port," laughed Jack. "That always seemed absurd to me, but there are lots of things that Verne wrote about which have been more than realized."

"I should say so! Why, his balloons and his submersibles would not be a patch upon what are actually in use these days."

"Well, now that we know it is safe here, and the water is not going to pour in upon us, let us have a look at the place," said Jack.

CHAPTER VII

A REMARKABLE FIND

The cabin where the boys now found themselves, so strangely lighted and so marvelously discovered, was not of any great size and was evidently the stateroom of the late commander of the vessel, which itself was not of any great size so far as the boys could determine.

It was furnished with a standing bed fixed against the side, a table and two chairs, all fixed to keep them from moving about when there was any commotion outside.

The skylight was just above the table, which could be used in writing or to have a meal served upon, there being evidences of its having been used for both purposes at the time of the wreck, for there were papers and writing materials scattered about, and a plate and a wine glass just under it, having fallen off during the commotion of the wreck.

There were lockers along the floor under the bed, and along the sides of the cabin, and in one corner a heavy chest such as seamen often use to contain their valuables, this being brassbound and padlocked.

There was a small door forward and another aft, but the boys did not attempt to see what was beyond either of them, being satisfied with what they saw, and not knowing what dangers they might bring upon themselves by doing so.

"It's a bit uncanny, Jack," murmured Percival, "having the water so near to us and not knowing at what moment it may come in upon us. One of those doors probably leads to the companionway going on deck, and the other to the cockpit, but I don't think it would be wise to open either."

"No," said Jack, picking up a bit of writing from the floor.

"There may be, and probably is, another door beyond this after one leading into the cockpit," pursued Percival, "but we don't know if we would let the water in upon us, and it is just as well to leave it alone for the present. The other doubtless leads to the companionway, and there may be another one beyond at the top or perhaps at the bottom. I don't see how the water has not made its way in here, but——"

"Both doors are of iron," said Jack. "Probably the skipper wanted privacy, and—do you read Spanish, Dick! You know a number of modern languages, more or less."

"No, not very well, but what made you ask me?" replied Percival in some surprise. "What have you got there, Jack?"

"A letter addressed to some official in Mexico, but whether of the provisional or rebel government I cannot make out."

"H'm! you are always picking up strange letters."

"Yes, it seems so. You are thinking of the one I found in the flying machine. We never settled whether that was really genuine or not, Dick, but this seems to be so. As far as I can make out it refers to a shipment of some sort, arms or gold or—why, Dick, this wreck cannot be so old, after all. The date of this is only that of last year and late at that."

"Then that knocks the Captain Kidd idea silly!"

"Never mind Captain Kidd. Let us see if we can open this chest. Do you know, I am a bit nervous about staying down here too long. You said it was uncanny, and so it is. I'll save these letters," picking up another from the floor. "Suppose we try the chest, Dick."

"The only reason that the water did not come in through that hole forward is that it was probably made by the rocks when she struck and this after part is much lower. She was caught fast and could not fall back. Well, what about the chest, can you open it?" for Jack was kneeling before it, and trying the fastenings.

"I don't know. The lock is closed, but it is only an ordinary iron one, and perhaps you might break it with the axe. There is no other lock that I can see. Try breaking it open, Dick."

Percival struck the padlock a terrific blow with the axe, and broke it in half, it being just a cast-iron affair and easily broken.

"It seems funny to put a lock like that upon a chest supposed to contain something worth while," remarked Jack, as he removed the pieces of the lock, pulled aside the hasp and opened the chest. "That is the way some persons do, however."

Throwing back the lid of the chest he found a tray containing some papers, a pair of pistols and a knife, a few odd trinkets of very little value, some loose cigarettes, two or three dozen in number, a cheap photograph, and a purse made of silver mesh containing a few gold coins.

"Whose picture is that, Dick?" he asked, handing the photograph to Percival, who took it and examined it carefully.

"Why, that's Villa or some of those rebel Mexicans," Dick answered. "I have seen it in the papers often. What's in the body of the chest?"

Jack removed the tray and set it on the floor, opening his eyes with astonishment, and giving vent to a startled exclamation at the same time.

"Well, it is not Captain Kidd, Dick," he cried, "but it is money, just the same, bags of it, and gold," untying the cord around one of the bags, and showing it to be full of gold pieces.

"Not pieces of eight, Jack?" asked Percival with a broad grin.

"No, American twenties and tens, and a few English sovereigns," said Jack, taking out a handful of the coins. "Why, there's more than a hundred dollars right in my fist."

"And a lot of bags, too, Jack," and Percival bent over and looked into the chest. "There must be thousands of dollars there, Jack."

"Yes, if they all contain gold. Take care of this one, Dick, while — —"

At that moment there was a sudden heavy sound outside, and both boys started up in surprise.

"What's that, Dick?"

"I don't know, but I don't like it."

"There is no water coming in?"

"Not that I can see."

The sound was repeated, louder than before, and Percival said nervously, while his cheek was noticed to have perceptibly paled:

"Let us get out of here, Jack. I am frightened, I admit. If anything should happen to you I would never forgive myself."

He closed the lid of the chest with his foot, caught Jack by the arm, and said as he hurried away:

"I don't know what it is, but I am not taking any risks."

They hurried along the passage by which they had entered the cabin, reached the hole in the bow by which they had entered and then, as Percival turned on his flashlight, which he had extinguished after entering the cabin aft, they hurried forward toward the hole in the rocks.

"There is no water here, Dick, at any rate," said Jack.

"No, there is not, but I can't think what made—hello!"

"What's the matter, Dick?"

"Where is the way up? I can't find it. The passage was not a wide one, was it? We cannot have gone astray?"

"No, I don't see how we could," muttered Jack, as he looked around him, the place being well lighted by Dick's flash. "Hello! I see what the trouble is, and now I know what the noise was."

"Well?" asked Percival.

"Some of the rocks have fallen in, Dick. That was what made the noise. Here is our rope. We are in the right place, therefore. The way up is closed, however. Or, at any rate, it is closed here, but I don't believe— —"

"The rocks were not loose, were they, Jack?"

"I did not notice that they were, and there has been no rain to send them down. They must have been loose, however. How else could they have tumbled in?"

"I don't know, unless some one took a bar or a pole, and sent them down that way."

"Nonsense, Dick! Who would do that?"

"I know plenty who would do it. Who pushed you into the ravine, back at Hilltop at the risk of your life?"

"Yes, but there is no one around, and no one knew where we were going. You don't suspect little Jesse W., do you?"

"No, indeed," said Percival, with a hearty laugh, "but some one has seen us go down here, and they have thrown down the rocks to make it harder for us to get out."

"It does not seem likely, Dick," said Jack in a doubting tone. "There was no one about, and we are the only ones who know the place. We said nothing about it, and young Smith will keep quiet. Come, that is hardly worth thinking of. Let us see how we can get out. There must be some way."

Dick turned his light this way and that, and Jack lighted a match, saying with a significant chuckle:

"That is all very well, but this is better for our purpose. Watch!"

The flame presently began to flicker, and indicated the presence of a draught of air, Jack noticing the direction whence it came, said:

"Try this way, Dick. There is a draught which makes the flame flicker. Try the axe on the rocks and see if you can loosen them, or, better yet, see if there isn't a fissure somewhere."

"Yes, there is," said Percival, climbing a mass of rock somewhat to one side of where the others had fallen. "Yes, I see it, Jack."

Between them, working with the axe and their hands, the boys opened up a passage between the rocks wide enough for them to crawl through, and in a few minutes were on the top of the wooded point only a few yards from where they had entered the strange place.

"The boat's gone, Jack!" exclaimed Percival.

CHAPTER VIII

DISCUSSING THE FIND

The boys could see the water and the bank from where they stood, and Dick had been the first to notice that the boat was not where they had left it before going down into the buried wreck.

"I suppose it might have drifted away," said Jack. "The warp could have become loosened."

"Yes, it could have done so," sputtered Percival, "but it did not do so without help. The same fellows who tumbled the rocks into the hole took away the boat. I have an idea who they were. I spoke pretty sharp to Herring the other day, and he has probably been nursing his wrath ever since."

"You are too suspicious, Dick, and—hello! did you bring that bag with you?" for the first time noticing that Percival had the bag of coin which he himself had handed to his friend.

"Yes, you told me to take care of it, and I did," and Percival put the bag in the outside pocket of his jacket. "Well have to hail the yacht, old chap. We can make our way in that direction along the top of the bank. It is not such bad going, and then we have the axe if it is necessary to cut our way through the undergrowth."

They set out along the top of the bank, keeping a lookout for the vessel, now and then having to cut their way on account of the thickness of the growth, which was often as high as their waists.

"The rocks could not have fallen in by themselves, and the boat gotten adrift at the same time," muttered Percival as they went on. "Both of these things were done by some one who wished to annoy us. Watch and see how some of the fellows look when we get back."

"Very well, I will, but I don't see why any one should have done it, perhaps both of these things were accidents."

"Either one of them might have been, but is it likely that both were, and that they happened at the same time? Of course not. You will find that Herring or Merritt, or perhaps both, have had a hand in it. They don't like you, and do everything to hurt you, and they don't care any more for me than they do for you. Bother this tangle! It keeps you busy every moment. I believe things grow up here in a night. There will be bare rocks one day and a regular forest on them the next. It beats all how things do grow in these tropical islands!"

Keeping on, now in sight of the water, and then having to leave it on account of the thickness of the jungle, they pushed on till they saw the yacht lying at anchor.

Descending to the shore at the risk of a bad fall, they hailed the vessel, and presently some one put out in a boat and came toward them.

Bucephalus and old Ben Bowline were in the boat, the old sailor hailing them when he neared the shore.

"Well, mateys, did you think you'd walk out to the yacht?" he asked. "The old man was afraid you'd fallen in, and been gobbled up by sharks. Some of the boys found the boat adrift, and brought it in. Don't you know how to tie up a boat yet? I'll show you some knots if you don't know them."

"We know all the knots you can show us, Ben, and perhaps a good many more," grunted Percival. "The boat was tied all right, but——"

"Wha' was yo' goin' to say, sah?" asked Bucephalus.

"Some one untied it," said Percival. "Who brought it back, Buck?"

"Ah donno, sah, Ah didn' saw dem, othahwise Ah could identify de pussons. Have yo' any ideah as to deir pussonality you'se'f, sah?"

"I have an idea, but ideas can't hang a man. Anyhow, I don't want it to get abroad that Jack Sheldon and I do not know how to tie up a boat or tie any ordinary kind of knot. The whole Academy would laugh at us if that notion got around."

"Ah reckon de 'cademy knows all abo't yo' an' Mistah Jack a'ready an' wha' yo' done befo' dis," said the negro with a broad grin. "Ah reckon, too, dat de story was a fabrication puah an' simple. Fact am, if Ah done tol' a story lak dat folks would call it a lie witho't mincin' wo'ds."

"That's about what it was," said Percival, as he and Jack got into the boat, and Bucephalus and Ben Bowline started to row them to the yacht.

"I had a comical adventure with a boat myself once, mateys, if you care to hear it," said old Ben as he bent leisurely upon his oar, "but maybe the young gentleman won't believe it."

"Go ahead, Ben, let's have it," spoke up Jack. "Never mind whether we believe it or not. It will amuse us at any rate."

"A sailor man is a mo' pribileged pusson dan one what resides on sho', Ah've noticed," observed Bucephalus. "Folks lak to listen to dem an' dey don' call it lyin', whereas an' on de oder han', ef Ah indulge in any picturesque adaptations o' de trufe dey say Ah'm lyin' right away."

"Never mind that," chuckled Percival. "There is no hurry and Ben wants to spin his yarn, so you might as well let him. Take it easy. There is no hurry. Go ahead, Ben."

The old sailor was a good deal mollified by Dick's present attitude, and taking an easy stroke with his oar, he began his more or less veracious narrative.

"It was down on the coast o' South Ameriky that this here thing happened, but I never had it put in the log 'cause the old man wasn't along an' nothin' went into it that he didn't see hisself; but it's just as true, I'm giving you my word——"

"As the one about the whale!" roared Dick. "Go on, Ben."

"We was sailin' along the coast o' South Ameriky," Ben went on, "when one day as I was cleanin' out one o' the boats to have ready when we went ashore, which we judged would be in a little while, there come up a sudden squall an' I was chucked clean overboard, boat and all.

"Davits, falls, blocks and everything went, and me too, striking the water kerplump. Then it got so dark that I couldn't see nothin', and where I was I had no idee, no more'n nothin', 'cause I couldn't see a thing and there was such a noise all around that I couldn't hear a thing. Then it come on to rain for further orders and I was just drenched to the skin and had all I could do to keep the boat bailed out.

"I couldn't see nor hear anything of the old hooker and I just drifted without knowin' where I was goin' and not carin' much nuther, bein' wet to the hide an' tired out with bailin' an' just ready to flop down an' quit.

"Well, I drifted an' drifted without knowin' where I was driftin', till finally I seen a shore at some distance off an' took the oars an' pulled for it, havin' somethin' to think of now.

"It was still a-rainin', but I didn't care for that now, but just pulled for shore till it got dark again and stopped rainin', which was a comfort. I pulled on till it was too dark to see anythin', and then I come to a stake stickin' out of the water and hitched my boat to it and lay in the bottom an' went right to sleep.

"As long as I was tethered to the stake or bush or whatever it was I reckoned I was all right, an' so I slep' on without feelin' a bit alarmed, knowin' that I wouldn't drift no more an' in the mornin' I could go on an' reach the shore.

"When I woke up in the mornin' I was mightily astonished to find myself lyin' on the ground at the foot of a big tree and to find the boat hangin' to the topmost limb. Ye see, the rainwater had run off an' left the ground bare again, and as the boat slipped down to the perpendickalar I was dropped out an' went from branch to branch till——"

Percival let out a hearty laugh and fairly shook himself, saying at last when he could find breath:

"Baron Munchausen with variations. I've heard that story before, Ben, but the rain was snow and the twig was a church steeple. Still, it's a good story and will bear a bit of a change."

"H'm! I knowed you'd say I was lyin'!" grunted Ben, pulling heartily on his oar and cutting his story short.

Dick put the bag of gold and the letters Jack had picked up in his trunk under his berth and locked it, saying nothing at that time to any one, but resolving to go again with Jack, and bring away the chest if they could manage it.

He meant to tell the doctor about their wonderful find when they had all of it safely in their possession, and to have the letters translated so as to learn definitely all about the wrecked vessel and its mission, but just now he thought it wise to say nothing and Jack agreed with him.

Not all of the boys were on the yacht when the two young adventurers returned, and nothing was said about their having to hail the yacht, but as the others began to arrive, some time later, Percival watched them in turn to see if he could distinguish guilty looks on the faces of any.

When Herring and Merritt came on board he suddenly stepped out from behind a funnel, which had hidden him so that the two bullies did not see him till just as he faced them.

Both of them showed surprise, and Percival said to himself:

"They are the ones, just as I supposed. When anything happens to me or Jack and especially to Jack, look out for Pete Herring."

The two bullies passed him as quickly as they could, and had nothing to say, being evidently much astonished at seeing him on the yacht, but fearing to say anything lest they should betray themselves.

Passing Percival they came suddenly upon Jack, not having time to prepare for a meeting with him, and both of them flushed crimson.

"Oh, then it was you who found the boat afloat and brought it back?" Jack said carelessly. "Very kind of you, I am sure."

"What boat, what are you talking about?" growled Herring, turning redder than ever. "I don't know nothing about no boats."

"No, I suppose not," laughed Jack carelessly, and then going on to join Percival, who said:

"Herring and Merritt are the fellows."

"Yes, so I supposed. They don't know anything about it. They never know anything about things that happen to me, and generally you cannot prove it on them."

"We can't now, but I am satisfied that they were in it just the same."

"Well, we got out of it all right, so there is no need of accusing them. The next time we go there we will be on the watch."

"I suppose they saw the boat, and then came up to see what we were doing, saw the rope and knew we were down in the hole, and closed it upon us."

"They might have drawn up the rope, but they don't think of everything, fellows like that."

"No, they do not, and that's how you can catch them."

Later Dick and Jack saw the captain and Dr. Wise in the cabin, and told about the wrecked schooner, as she probably was, and of the visit to the cabin under water, and the finding of the gold.

Dick exhibited the bag Jack had given him, and showed the letters found on the floor, the captain being able to read them.

"There were money and supplies shipped to the Mexican rebel leader," he said, "and probably the vessel may have been chased, and put in among the islands of the Caribbean to get away, and was wrecked here. There is quite a lot of money in this bag, about a thousand dollars, and if there are many of the bags and they are all as full as this, you will have a pretty good sum to dispose of."

"The money belongs to Jack," said Percival. "He discovered the wreck and it should be his. He needs the money, and I do not."

"You worked with me," put in Jack, "and if I have any of it you should have a share. Does it belong to us, however?"

"Of course it does," said Captain Storms. "You found it and that's the law of treasure trove. It isn't likely that the Mexican rebels or their agents will put in a claim for it, and it is yours all right."

"But we have not got the rest of it," said Jack, "and the hold might be flooded before we go there again. It is a wonder that the water has kept out as long as it has."

"The iron doors have done a lot to keep it out; they are probably watertight. That cabin you were in was like a strong room, and maybe the skipper had it built that way a purpose. You don't know what sort of crew you may get when you are on a lay of this sort, and I guess he wasn't taking chances, having a lot of money on board."

"That may account for it, but it made me feel a little creepy being in there, and knowing that the water was just above me, and perhaps on the other side of those doors."

"I don't wonder. They say divers get afraid when they see all sorts of fishes swimming around them under water. I'd like to go to the place with you. I've had some queer adventures, but nothing so queer as that."

"I should be very glad to have you, sir, and if you want a share of the money in the chest— —"

"No, that's all right. It belongs to you and your friend and the little fellow, too, I suppose."

"Why, of course, they must have their share of it."

"I don't think Jesse W. will take it, and, anyhow, he was not with us when we went into the cabin, and I certainly don't want it," said Percival. "It all belongs to you, Jack."

"Not if I don't want to take it," Jack replied with a laugh. "How are you going to make me take it, Dick?"

"I'm sure I don't know, but it ought to be yours, just the same. I'd like to get the rest of it, and suppose we go after it to-morrow?"

"That will be all right."

"And I'll go along to help you," said the captain. "There's no getting out of here right away, and we may as well do something. I can't get any answer to my wireless messages yet, and maybe folks think they're only a joke, and don't pay any attention."

"You have tried to get New York?" asked Jack.

"Yes, and Havana and any place I can, but I can't do anything. I don't know if I am tuned up with those fellows or whether they think it is only a joke or what. I've tried American and International, wired S.O.S. and all the different distress signals, but could not seem to make connection."

"Why don't you try Mr. Smith in New York? He would be interested on account of his boy. Try a plain commercial message. That ought to go. You can at least try it."

"That is very sensible advice," said the doctor. "I suppose you have been sending out distress signals, and the wireless people, if they have caught you up simply regard it as a hoax."

"Well, I'll try again, and do as the young man suggests. In the meantime I'd like to visit this wreck. I never was in a ship's cabin under water when it was safe, and I'd like to try it."

"We will go to-morrow," said Jack.

CHAPTER IX

THE LAST VISIT TO THE WRECK

The next day, as agreed upon, they went to the old wreck on the rocks to get more of the treasure in the hold, and to satisfy the captain's curiosity about the place.

It had gotten around among the boys that Jack and Dick had found a sunken treasure, and there were stories of fabulous wealth afloat in a short time, all the boys, with a few exceptions, wishing to visit the place and gaze upon the buried gold with their own eyes.

"We cannot have all those boys visiting the place and getting in our way," sputtered Percival when it was suggested by Harry that he and one or two others go with the party.

"But we would not be in the way," said young Dickson, "and we might be of assistance."

"How did you find it out anyhow?" asked Percival. "We did not say anything about it."

"I don't know, but, at any rate, it is all around, and everybody knows about it. I heard Herring talking about it. He seems to think it is a big hoax, and that you did not find anything."

"Well, we did, all the same, but we don't want a lot of fellows with us, and, besides, it is dangerous. Never mind, Hal. You are in with us on the most of our adventures, but I don't think you had better go this time. We have promised to take young Jesse W. with us, as he was there the first time, but not the second, and he has never seen the cabin with its strange lights, the swash of water outside, the chest of gold and all that."

"H'm! you make me want to go with you all the more," said Harry, half laughing, half impatient. "You should not appeal to a boy's imagination like that, Dick. I want to go with you now the worst way."

"Well, I suppose you do, but you'll have to be satisfied with what I tell you about it. I'll write a composition about it, and you will think you are reading Jules Verne and the Arabian Nights all over again."

"You be smothered!" sputtered Harry, half cross and half good natured. "As if that would satisfy me."

"It will have to, Hal," laughed Percival. "Never mind, I'll give you a ten-dollar gold piece to hang on your watch chain as a charm. You can say it was one that Captain Kidd had."

"Yes, and they were not made at that time, two hundred years ago," said Harry in disgust. "Well, never mind. Billy Manners and I will find a buried treasure, and never let you have a smell of it"

"All right, Harry," and Dick went away to get Jack, young Smith and the captain, and start on their visit to the point.

The captain had a rope and an axe, and Jack took his pocket flash along with him, having found it very useful on the second visit to the submerged vessel.

They climbed up the rocks, and found the place where they had gone down, but now the opening was so small, more rocks having fallen in, apparently, since their last visit, that they doubted if they could get down.

"I am afraid we shall have to give it up," said Jack in some disappointment. "The last time Dick and I were here we had to squeeze through to get out, but now it seems worse than before."

"Let me try, Jack," said young Smith eagerly. "I am only a little fellow, and can get through where big fellows like you and Dick could not. Don't you remember how you put me through the little window at the Academy, that time of the rebellion in the school? Well, you can use me now in the same way. I want to see that place down there. You know I did not see it the last time, and I want to see it very much. Try, Jack. I am not so big, and can squeeze through almost anywhere."

Jack found a place where it would be quite possible for Jesse W. to get down, but not for himself or Percival, and, of course, out of the question for the captain, who was nearly as big as both of the latter combined, and he said:

"Here is a place, J.W., which, I think, will fit. It does seem too bad that you should not see the place, having been with us on our first trip, and we will give you a chance."

"I can bring away a bagful of the gold, anyhow, Jack, and perhaps go for another one after that. I should like to see the place, anyhow."

"All right, you shall do so, old man, but don't load yourself down with gold. That has drowned many a man before now. Get the rope, Dick. We will lower him into the place. Take a light, Jesse W., for you will need it. You know just how to find everything?"

"Yes, I go into the hole in the bow of the vessel which we saw, follow along till I come to a door, and then go along a passage till I come to another door and there I am, right in the cabin with a light overhead, shining through the water."

"That's it. Don't stay too long, and don't load yourself down with bags of gold. I'd rather not have it than have you take any risks."

"But you don't think there is any danger, Jack?" asked the younger boy, as they prepared to lower him.

"No, if I did I would not let you go."

The boy got down safely enough, and called to Jack and Dick when he had reached the bottom that he was all right, and then threw off the rope, which had been put around him under his arms.

He called to them from time to time, his voice growing fainter every time he called, and at last they could not hear him at all.

"I hope it is all right," murmured Jack when the boy had been gone a few minutes. "I thought it would be when I let him go, but now — —"

"It is all right," said the captain. "He is a plucky little fellow, and there isn't anything that can happen to him. The rocks hold the vessel as tight as a vise and there is no chance of her slipping back into the water or anything of that sort."

"Well, I hope so, but somehow I begin to feel nervous, and wish that I had not let him go down."

"Young Smith is all right, Jack," said Percival reassuringly. "He is not afraid of anything, and really I don't believe there is anything to be afraid of. There was not when we went down."

"No, but we are a couple of big boys, and he is only a midget. If anything happened to him I should never forgive—listen, and see if you can hear him coming."

"No, I cannot, but he has had hardly time to get there yet. Give him a chance. He will want to see all there is, boy-like. Let him have a good long look at the wonders of the place. He has never seen anything like it before, and never will again."

Jack was very anxious in spite of Dick's cheering words, and the minutes seemed like hours till at last, holding the rope in his hand he felt a tug at, and then heard:

"Hello! Are you up there?"

"Yes!" shouted Jack. "Are you all right?"

"Sure I am. Wait till I get the rope under my arms. I've got a bag of the stuff, as I said I would, but I don't think——"

"You don't think what?" asked Jack, thinking that he detected something in the tone of the boy's voice that indicated danger of some sort.

"Nothing, wait till I get the rope fast."

"Very good. Take your time."

"All right," the boy called in a few moments. "I have got it. Haul away!"

They saw the light of the electric torch flashing upon them, as the boy came nearer and nearer to them, and at last drew him out of the hole, Jack noticing that he seemed quite pale, and then suddenly noticing that he was wet up to his knees.

"Hello! what is this, Jesse W., how do you happen to be so wet?" he asked. "There was no water in— —"

"Yes, some," answered the boy quietly. "It had worked in under the door or at the side somewhere. Maybe they had settled. Anyhow, I got the bag and here it— —" and then the boy sank limp and helpless into Jack's arms and fainted away.

"By George! he was a plucky little fellow and no mistake!" exclaimed Jack. "He said that he would get the bag and he did, and standing in water up to his knees, and not knowing at what time he might have the whole Caribbean sea tumbling in upon him. Get some water, Dick!"

The boy presently came around, however, and said faintly, but with a half laugh:

"I told you I'd bring it, didn't I, Jack? Well, I did, and I hope it will be enough to keep you at the Academy for the rest of the course. If it isn't, my father— —"

"You are a brave young fellow, Jesse W., but you don't go back for another, I tell you that!"

"You bet he does not!" echoed Percival. "So the water had made its way in, had it? That's the last we will see of the place, then."

"Yes, it had come in somewhere, at the bottom, I guess. Still, it was not coming in all the time nor fast, and I wanted to see the place, and I had promised to fetch a bag of gold to Jack and— —"

"And you wanted to keep your word even if you were drowned," sputtered Percival. "Much you could have kept it in that case. You are a young brick, J.W., but don't you do anything like that again."

"Well, I won't, if you say so, Dick," answered the little fellow.

"That's a brave little chap," said the captain. "He said he'd do a thing, and he did it. There's lots who wouldn't."

They returned to the boat, and the captain told Percival to row toward the reefs and as close to the stump of a mast as it was safe to go, as he wanted to observe the wreck again.

Nearing the wreck they noticed that the water was swirling and eddying very violently at a point where they judged the cabin to be, and the captain said, after looking at the boiling waters for a short time:

"The water is making its way in and will run forward as far as its level. She'll break up with all that water in her, and I wouldn't be surprised to see her go any time."

In fact as they lay there watching the boiling waters over the sunken vessel, they saw them become more greatly agitated and Percival pulled away to a safer distance as the agitation increased.

Then of a sudden the stump of a mast sank into the water, there was a still greater agitation and a mass of broken timbers shot up into the air and then fell back, and went floating away on the tide.

"That's about the last of her," said Captain Storms, "or, at any rate, you won't go into the cabin again. You've made your last visit to the wreck, and if any one ever gets that money he'll have to dive for it. You can be thankful that you went there when you did."

"So I am," said Jack. "Come on, Dick, pull away from here."

CHAPTER X

A THRILLING ENCOUNTER

Returning to the yacht first for the captain to get aboard, Jack and Percival then took the boat and went to the outer bay on a little exploring trip of their own, the rest not caring to make any more explorations at that time.

The boys guided the boat along shore not too near the rocks, both keeping watch for any nook which might prove of interest or afford an opportunity for an adventure of any sort.

There was a short, keen-bladed hatchet to cut their way through the thicket if necessary when they went ashore, and Percival had a rifle with which to shoot any game they might come across, both being placed on one of the forward thwarts.

Jack was provided with his pocket flashlight in case they went into dark places, and Dick had a revolver in his pocket, declaring that this might be of as much use as the torch in case they came to close quarters with an enemy, no matter of what sort.

As they were rowing at a lazy rate, keeping up a slow, even stroke, Jack, who was keeping a lookout on the shore and steering at the same time, suddenly said, looking toward a mass of rocks which they had just come abreast:

"There looks to be a sort of cave in there, Dick. At any rate, there is a hole which seems to run in to some little distance. Suppose we explore it and see how far we can go."

"I'm in for anything that you are, Jack," replied Dick.

"All right, pull ahead, not too fast, and we'll have a look at the place."

"Pull ahead it is, Jack."

Jack was in the bow and he now steered the boat toward the opening in the rocks, which was quite big enough for them to enter, and they went on at a slow, steady gait, presently gliding into the water cave, for such it seemed, with plenty of room above and on both sides.

Jack turned his head now and then to see how they were progressing and if there were any obstructions in the way, and presently said:

"A little slower, Dick. It is getting darker in here now and I do not want to run into anything."

"Slower it is, Jack. It would not be any fun to stave a hole in the bottom of the boat. It doesn't belong to us."

"That would be reason enough for not daring, with some persons," said Jack with a low laugh. "They will take care of their own things, but are careless with those belonging to others."

"The woods are full of such, Jack."

Jack rowed with one hand, drawing in his other oar so that it might not strike the rocks in case the passage narrowed, and then got out his pocket flash and shot a strong ray ahead of him.

"Good gracious! what's that?" suddenly exclaimed Percival in accents of terror. "Back water, Jack, for heaven's sake!"

"What is it, Dick?" asked Jack, turning his head and sending the light directly in front of him. "I don't see anything."

"It's gone, Jack, or the light does not strike it now, but it was something awful. It fairly gave me the creeps to look at it."

"But what was it, Dick?" and Jack slowly turned the light this way and that so as to get a sight at the object which had so terrified Percival.

"I don't know. It had two awful eyes and a beak and a lot of legs, or arms, or whatever they were, and a fat body which—there it is, Jack!"

Jack saw it and shuddered.

"It's a devil fish, an octopus, Dick," he muttered, turning the light now full upon the grisly object squatting on a rock at the farther end of the water cave and glaring balefully at the boys through his blood-red eyes, like some demon of the deep, the very mention of which might send terror to the bravest hearts.

"We'd better get out quick, Jack!" gasped Percival. "If that fellow——"

What he might have said was cut short by a sudden splash in the water which caused the boat to rock violently and dashed the spray in their faces.

Then there was a whip-like sound and Jack felt himself struck by something which quickly wound itself about one arm and a part of his body and swiftly pulled him out of the boat.

He dropped his flashlight, but as he left the boat his free arm swung out and his hand touched something which he seized in an instant.

It was the short hatchet on the thwart and he had seized it by the helve, well up toward the top.

With the swiftness of thought itself he realized what had happened.

The octopus had wound one of its tentacles about his arm and body and, clinging to them with a tenacity which he could not overcome, had pulled him out of the boat.

Percival gave a scream of fright as Jack went overboard, although he was usually a very self-contained young fellow and not apt to give way to hysterical outbreaks.

It was dark in the cave, but he quickly groped for the torch which Jack had dropped, and cried out:

"Where are you, Jack? What has happened?"

Jack went under water and felt himself being drawn toward the end of the water cave where he had seen the octopus squatting on the rock.

His thoughts flew like lightning and, being a resourceful boy, he instantly decided what to do.

He had kept his breath from a natural instinct and now with his free arm he dealt a swinging blow with the little axe in a direction which would not cause him to injure himself but might strike the clinging tentacle.

His one hope was that another of the flying arms might not reach him and secure his other arm, which fortunately was his right.

He suddenly felt a resistance and realized that he had struck something and hoped that it might be the tentacle of the octopus.

In another moment he felt the pressure on his arm and body relax and then realized that something had fallen from them.

He struck out vigorously with both arms, the pressure upon his lungs from having held his breath so long beginning to be unbearable.

Then he felt his right arm seized, the suckers on the tentacle pressing strong upon his muscles and seeming to draw the blood even under his clothing, and he knew that the baleful creature had again gotten a hold upon him.

He was able to clutch the hatchet in his left hand as the power gave out in his right, and at that moment he arose to the surface and drew a succession of deep breaths before another of those terrible arms seized him by the leg and drew him again under water.

In another instant, as he struck wildly at the eldritch creature that held him and felt the tension on his arm relax, everything became suddenly black.

The octopus had resorted to one of its natural tricks and had ejected a dense black fluid into the water which made it impossible for him to see anything.

The creature was drawing him toward some hole in the cave, probably under water, and he realized most poignantly that something must be done shortly or he would be sacrificed to the pitiless water devil.

He felt himself rising and in a moment, when he most needed it, was able to get his breath.

The devil fish, even with the loss of two of its arms, was still powerful enough to make all his efforts futile, and he felt himself being drawn into some recess beyond where he had first seen the octopus squatting on the rock and glaring at them with its horrible eyes.

Percival, having found Jack's electric torch and searching the cave below and above water for a sign of his friend, suddenly saw the devil fish rise to the ledge where he had first seen it.

Jack was now caught in two of its remaining arms and was being drawn toward some deep recess whence there would be no rescuing him.

Transferring the light to his left hand, Percival whipped out the revolver from his hip pocket with his right and took rapid aim.

"I'm afraid it will be like trying to pierce an elephant's hide," he muttered, "but I'm going to try it for all that."

Luckily he caught sight of the creature's eyes at the moment and took aim straight for one of them.

Jack was being drawn toward the horrible beak and the sight nearly unnerved Dick.

Fortunately he had aimed and pressed the trigger before he saw this ghastly sight.

He fired three or four shots in quick succession and then heard the sound of a plunge in the water.

Jamming his torch into the clutch of one of the tholepins, he seized the rifle and shot a quick glance ahead of him.

Jack was not to be seen, but he did see the octopus writhing and waving its frightful arms on the ledge.

"Where are you, Jack?" he shouted.

"All right!" cried Jack himself, rising just alongside the boat and holding on to the gunwale with one hand.

"I'll finish that demon before he can do any more mischief!" hissed Dick.

It was Jack falling into the water that had caused the plunge he had heard and not the return of the octopus to its element.

Now, taking quick but careful aim, Percival fired half a dozen shots from the repeating rifle he had seized and with deadly effect.

The revolver shots had wounded the octopus, but not fatally, and he might at any moment plunge into the water and seize Jack.

The heavier caliber weapon did the work.

As Jack climbed into the boat there was a great plunge into the water which caused the light craft to rock again and the spray to fly.

"That settles him!" gasped Percival, and then he dropped his weapon and drew Jack into the boat, where he promptly sank limp and helpless under the thwarts, all his strength having seemingly left him.

"All right, Jack?" asked Percival.

"Yes, but get away," answered Jack feebly.

Percival was not slow to obey the injunction.

Seizing the oars, he quickly backed water and then turned the head of the boat toward the entrance of the cave, whence he shortly saw the light streaming in as he pulled a quick, powerful stroke.

"I'm glad that's over!" he said with a sigh of deep relief as he neared the opening. "No more exploring queer places like this again!"

When he was outside the cave he rested on his oars and said:

"You are all right again, Jack?"

"Yes," said Jack, getting up and seating himself on a thwart, "but I don't want another such an experience. I feel as if all the blood had been drawn out of me by that horrible thing in there."

Out in the bright sunlight, away from the gruesome cave and its dreadful tenant, Jack seemed to recover his spirits quickly, however, and he presently took one of the oars and then another, and said:

"It's all right, Dick. We are away from the horrible thing and I thank heaven I am still alive to tell of it. Let us go somewhere else."

"Right you are, I will," echoed Percival heartily. "If I had had any idea that there was such a thing in that place you could not have hired me to go into it or to have let you ventured there. I am glad enough that I was around to be of assistance."

"So am I, Dick, but suppose we say no more about it. I hate to even think of the horrible object and I only hope that I will not dream of it these nights."

Then the boys rowed swiftly away from the place where they had had such a thrilling encounter and never once looked back at it.

CHAPTER XI

THE VOICES IN THE WOODS

After the boys had gone some little distance from the water cave they pulled at a more easy stroke and began to talk again, their thrilling experience with the devil fish having made them silent for a time.

They did not allude to it again, but talked of other matters, Percival saying as they neared a green, shady wood where the trees grew thick and cast a deep shade on the white sands and showed a more than twilight darkness in their farther recesses, everything being quiet and peaceful within those heavy shadows:

"That's a place where everything seems to be asleep even at midday, Jack. It looks like the cave of the seven sleepers that we used to read about in mythology."

"It seems quiet enough for a fact," said Jack with a smile, "but it is hot outside and the birds are probably all taking a rest. Probably just before dawn or at sunset you would hear them making noise enough."

"It is a thick wood all right, just the place to get lost in. If the African jungle is any worse than this I don't care to enter it."

"The trouble is you can't see far ahead and then there are briars and brambles and a lot of spiky plants, prickly pears and Spanish bayonets and cactus to run against and get scratched and cut with. Our own woods are good enough for me, or bad enough, I might say."

"I wonder if we could find anything if we did go in there?" said Percival musingly as they rowed along shore, fascinated by the bright glare of the sands, the dense green of the woods and the dear blue of the skies. "We might have a try at it, Jack."

"Yes, I suppose we might if we did not go too — —" And then Jack suddenly paused and a look of alarm came across his face.

A harsh voice from the wood suddenly interrupted him and he glanced here and there to see whence it came.

The words he heard were in Spanish, as far as he could judge, but he could see no one.

Other voices quickly joined the first and the boys rowed out somewhat from shore and looked closely at the woods, expecting to see some one.

"There are people on the island after all, Jack."

"Yes, Spaniards, I think. Sailors, I guess. At any rate they are not using the choicest language from what little I know of the language; Jack. I do not see any one. Do you?"

There were loud and angry voices in the woods, but the boys could see no one and went on slowly, farther out from shore so as to be out of danger in case any one appeared.

"A lot of drunken sailors would not be good company," declared Jack. "I would rather be alone."

"It can't be any one from the yacht, can it?"

"No, I don't think so. We have no Spaniards and Captain Storms brings his men up better than that. Besides, if it were some of our men we would see a boat, and there is nothing."

They still heard the voices at intervals as they rowed on and had no desire to enter the woods as long as the men were there.

"That's a nuisance," said Percival with a half-growl as they rowed on. "I would have liked to go ashore there, but of course if there are a lot of swearing Spaniards hanging about it wouldn't do."

"I'd like to know what brought them here," remarked Jack. "We got in by the sheerest good luck and it does not seem possible that another vessel could have done the same. Those things don't happen twice."

"Well, they are here, at all events, and it stops our going ashore. I'd like to know if they saw us in the boat?"

"I don't suppose so. They did not show themselves and they would not have made so much noise if they had——"

Just then the voices were heard again and the boys stopped rowing.

"There they are again!" muttered Percival. "We may have trouble, Jack."

The voices were very loud and the language used was not of the choicest, although, being in Spanish, it was not as offensive as it would have been in English, the boys not understanding much of what was said.

"Are they quarreling, do you suppose?" asked Percival.

"No, I don't think so," and Jack suddenly laughed.

"What are you laughing at?" asked Percival, somewhat impatiently.

"Listen a minute, Dick," said Jack.

The voices had ceased, but presently they were heard again, closer than before, and then a big, gorgeously feathered parrot flew out of a clump of trees not ten feet from shore.

"There are your quarrelsome Spaniards, Dick," laughed Jack, as another parrot joined the first.

"Well, I declare!" laughed Dick. "Are you sure, Jack?"

"Yes. The first time I heard them I was deceived, but just now I fancied there was something queer about those voices and I decided that there were parrots in the woods."

"Yes, but Jack, Spanish is not the natural language of parrots and they must have heard it from men. That proves that there are men on the island."

"Or that there have been, at any rate, but we don't know that there are any here at present."

"Well, as long as we know that there is nothing more dangerous than a lot of parrots, suppose we go ashore and look about a bit."

They found a good landing place where there was a shelving beach extending for some distance in either direction, and a clump of trees close to the water, where they tied the warp of the boat to keep it from floating away.

They saw more of the parrots, but not all of them imitated the human talk, chattering and making harsh sounds after their own fashion and making the glades bright with their gorgeous plumage.

Both boys laughed at the recollection of their first fright when they heard the birds and thought that there were men on the island, and then, taking their bearings, set out to explore the island for a short distance.

As Jack had a good idea of direction, they were not likely to get lost, although in the jungle they were often in a twilight shade and could not see the sun, which might have told them which way they were going.

"It gave me something of a start when I thought there were other people on the island besides ourselves," remarked Percival as they went on through a semi-darkness, the vegetation being thick above and around them so that they could see nothing of the sky. "It's pretty dark here."

"Yes," agreed Jack, turning on his pocket flash. "Hello!"

"What's the matter?" asked Percival, Jack's tone being one of alarm.

A shot rang out, and then Jack jumped back, exclaiming:

"I guess I've settled him, Dick!"

"What have you settled, Jack?"

"That fellow there," and Jack turned the light upon something at his feet and then pushed it aside.

"A snake!" exclaimed Percival. "You blew his head off. Is he very dangerous, Jack?"

"Well, not now," said the other with a dry laugh.

"No, I should say not. Would he have been?"

"He belongs to the family of dangerous snakes, one of the most dangerous, in fact. He is either a fer de lance or a first cousin to it, and either is a sort of creature to keep away from. The bite is nearly always fatal, as the virus acts so rapidly upon the system. It was lucky I turned on the light when I did. These creatures inhabit the dark places and are always ready for an unwary traveler."

"H'm! I think we had better keep in the light, Jack. We go into a dark water cave and run across a devil fish. Then we go into the dark woods and meet with this poison gentleman. Let's go back to the light!"

"I think we had better," returned Jack. "We are strangers here and the residents seem to resent our coming. I am sure I'll be glad enough to leave the place for good."

It did not seem to be such an easy matter, however, for difficulties beset them on every side as soon as they started to leave the jungle, as though there were some malign influence in those gloomy shades which was endeavoring to hold them captive.

There were morasses which they had to avoid, there were bramble thickets which barred their way, and Percival questioned whether Jack was going in the right direction and asked him to try another.

"We are going toward the shore, Dick," said Jack, "and if we keep on you will see that I am right."

"I don't doubt that we were going that way in the beginning, Jack, but we were thrown out of our path by the brambles and again by the swamp, not to mention the snake, and I don't believe we are going that way now. Don't the trees give you any idea?"

"Yes, and I am sure we are going toward the water. If we had a bit of daylight I could convince you, but it is as dark as a pocket here. I never saw trees grow so thick."

Jack had his way, for Percival had confidence in him and at length the boy paused and said:

"Listen, Dick! There are the parrots again. They won't talk if it is dark and all we have to do is to follow the sound and we will shortly come out into the light."

"I guess you're right," laughed the other. "I know we always used to cover our bird with a dark cloth when it got to chattering too much, and it stopped in an instant. But I don't hear them."

"Listen!" said Jack, pressing forward by the light of his pocket torch.

"I hear them now," said Percival. "They are using as bad language as ever. Those are educated parrots, although their education has not been of the best."

In a short time they heard the parrots much plainer than before and then it grew lighter and still lighter till at length they were able to see the sky overhead through the branches and finally the sun itself, by which time they were right among the parrots, who were making a tremendous chattering.

"Well, we are obliged to you at any rate, even if you are a noisy lot," laughed Percival. "You frightened us first and then you showed us the way to the light. Still, are we in the right direction, Jack?"

"Certainly," and pushing on, Jack led the way into more open ground and in a short time they came in sight of the inner bay where the vessel lay at anchor.

"We are not so far out of our way, Dick," said Jack. "The boat lies just on the other side of that clump of trees and we can reach it in a few minutes."

He proved to be correct and, getting in, the boys rowed back to the yacht, where they amused and interested a party of their companions by telling of their adventures.

"Well, it is certainly not safe to go far away from the vessel," declared Billy Manners, "and I think if I do I will be sure to take Jack along as a guide."

"Not very complimentary to me," said Percival dryly.

"Oh, you want your own way too much."

"H'm! if I had had it we would have been lost yet, so I guess you are out there, William."

"Well, that only proves what I said in the first place," said Billy with a chuckle.

CHAPTER XII

ADVENTURES IN THE WOODS

One day not so long afterwards the boys returned to shore, but at a different place than they had been before, and set out on a walk through the woods toward the hill, which they had never managed to get to before, although they had tried it more than once.

They took the axe along, not knowing but they might want it, and set out in high spirits.

Hearing voices ahead of them they pushed on, and soon came across the old sailor, Ben Bowline, and the acting head cook, Bucephalus, discussing some knotty point.

"Ah tell yo' dis am not de way," said the negro in a very positive tone, "an' any one what has any perspicuity in his haid will tell yo' so."

"I don't know what that 'ere is, and I don't believe I ever had any, but it ain't the right road 'cordin' to the course," returned the sailor. "We sot out nothe-nothe-east, and this here course is due nothe, which ain't at all proper."

"Which way yo' wan' to go, Sailorman?" asked Buck.

"This here way, of course," said Ben, pointing.

"Huh! an' there ain't no path there, nothin' but briahs an' big rocks an' swamp. How yo' goin' to get through there? This here way is the right way, because it am plain to be seen that it am a thoroughfare, and has been promenaded by pedestrians before now."

"I don't care what has happened to it, and it may be a good road all the same, but it ain't the course we sot out on, and so it's the wrong one to take, and I ain't going to take it."

At this point Jack, Dick and Jesse W. came along, being much amused at the arguments offered by the disputants.

"How are you heading, Ben?" asked Jack in the soberest fashion.

"Nothe-nothe-east, sir," said the old seaman, saluting.

"Change your course to north."

"Aye-aye, sir, north it is," said Ben.

"And follow in our wake in case you are needed."

"Aye-aye, sir, follow in your wake it is, yes, sir."

"You could not have persuaded that grizzled old tar that there was any course but the one he started on, no matter what the difficulties of his course were, but give him a new one, and he will take it without the least question. That's the sailor of it."

"And they would have stood there arguing till the cows came home," said Dick. "You settled it in a moment."

"And if we need them they are there."

They kept on, now in the open and now in deep shade, having occasionally to cut their way, pushing on toward the hill, which Jack had determined to get to the top of, and now and then seeing it when they reached higher and more open ground.

They reached the top at length, and had a fine view of the island and of the sea, but could not see any other islands in the distance.

"We are on a lost island and no mistake," said Percival. "There is not another one in sight. I wish I could make out a passage through the reefs, but there does not seem to be any."

"We may find one unexpectedly," said Jack. "That often happens. You hunt and hunt for a thing and don't find it, and then you give up hunting and the first thing you know you find what you have been looking for without looking for it."

"That sounds like a contradiction," laughed Percival, "but I know what you mean."

Leaving the hill after getting a good view of the surrounding sea and the island, the boys took a course which would lead them to the part of the reefs, which they had not before visited.

They were pushing on leisurely when they suddenly stopped and listened, having heard what seemed to be a cry for help.

"Somebody is in trouble," said Jack. "Where is it, straight ahead?"

"It sounds like it, and that sounds like the voice of Billy Manners."

"Maybe he is joking," said young Smith. "He always is."

Just now came a lusty cry for help in so serious and agonized a tone that Jack said with a smile:

"Billy is not joking now, that is certain. He is in real trouble. Come on and let us see what it is."

They pushed on rapidly, the call being presently repeated, and at the same time they heard a bellowing sound, which they could not make out.

"Come on!" cried Percival. "Billy is in trouble, and that sounds like the bellow of a wild beast."

"I should say it was a calf," remarked Jesse W., "if you were to ask me about it, but what a calf is doing here——"

He hurried on to keep up with Jack and Dick, Buck and Ben following quickly, having evidently heard the noises.

Coming in a short time into an open space the boys paused and then began to laugh heartily, something they would certainly not have done if Billy had been in danger.

There, in the crotch of a little tree about six feet from the ground, was Billy Manners, while at the foot of the tree was a calf a few months' old bellowing lustily and evidently calling for food.

"I told you it was a calf!" laughed young Smith.

"Help!" roared Billy, seeing the boys. "Here is a wild bull, and I am treed. Shoot him, boys, drive him away, anything!"

Instead of doing anything the boys only stood there and laughed, and when Bucephalus and Ben Bowline came up in great haste they did the same, all joining in a full-voiced laughing chorus.

"Why don't you help a fellow?" wailed Billy. "There you all are, laughing to beat the band, and I can't get down on account of this wild bull at the foot of the tree."

"Wild bull nothing!" exclaimed Percival. "It is a three months' old calf, and you're another, only you are a bit older than that. Can't you tell a calf when you see one, or have you been brought up in the city where they don't have them except in the way of veal cutlets?"

"That a calf?" asked Billy in disgust. "I thought it was a wild bull. He makes noise enough."

"Probably calling for its mother," laughed young Smith. "I said it was a calf right along."

"Shoo!" said Buck, advancing on the terrible wild bull, which had so frightened Billy. "Get o't o' dat or Ah cut yo' up fo' de young ge'men's dinnah. Shoo!"

The calf let out a tremendous bellow, and scampered off into the woods, whereat the boys laughed harder than ever till the tears fairly ran down their cheeks.

"That's a good one on Billy who is all the time getting off jokes on other folks," said Percival. "That is too good to keep."

"Dick Percival," said Billy, laughing in spite of himself, "if you say a word about it I'll cut you dead."

"I can't help it," chuckled Dick; "it's too good to keep, and I won't keep it, no matter what are the consequences. Think of a boy who has spent the biggest part of his life in the country not knowing the difference between a little three months' old heifer calf and a wild bull. Billy, my boy, you have neglected your opportunities."

Billy got down from the tree, and all hands laughed again, but Jack said thoughtfully:

"That was not a wild calf, and the question naturally arises, what is a domesticated calf doing on a supposedly uninhabited island? If there is a calf there must be a cow and if a cow, then people who own and take care of her. There must be people on the island after all, although we have never seen them."

"We have not been all over the island," said Percival, "and it is likely that in the very parts where we have not been we shall find the people who own the calf."

"They are probably negroes or halfbreeds," added Jack, "and seldom visit the shore. Suppose we keep on. We may find a village, or, at any rate, one or two houses occupied by them. Come on, Billy, you are safer with us in case we come across another wild bull."

"Get out!" said Billy, half laughing, half in disgust. "How much will you take to keep quiet on that subject?"

"I could not think of making a bargain, Billy," chuckled Jack, "and then I am afraid it would cost you too much. Remember, there are myself and Dick, Jesse W. Smith, Bucephalus Johnson and Ben Bowline to be bought off, and the prices might go up."

"All right," muttered Billy with a wry face, "but don't rub it in too much, that's all."

"All right, I won't, but remember when you feel like playing jokes on the boys that I may say something about it."

"All right, but I say, what about it, that calf is not wild?"

"Not a bit of it, she is just as tame as any barn-yard calf along the Hudson valley. Calves are the same the world over."

"And Billy was one not to know it," said Percival with a grin. "Remember, William, you have not bought me off yet. I have made no promises, and neither has Jesse W. Smith."

"Oh, I don't care anything about it," said the smaller boy. "I won't say anything about it no matter how much Billy jokes, I am interested in the other matter. If there are tame calves here there must be more or less civilized people living on the island."

"Well, we have made two or three very good discoveries on our island," observed Percival. "We have found treasure, and we have found calves, and probably inhabitants."

"And the next thing is to find a way through the reefs," said Jack.

"If we found the others why should we not find that?" asked Percival. "We did not expect to find anything, and we have found a lot."

"But we won't find our way home," said Billy, "if we don't start pretty soon, for it will be dark in a little while."

"The funny fellow grows serious once in a while," chuckled Dick, "but I think he is right for all that."

"I think we had better be going myself," said Jack. "Ben Bowline?"

"Sir to you, sir," said the seaman.

"Steer south, and go on a free wind at four miles."

"Aye-aye, sir!" said Ben, and they all set out for home, as they called the yacht.

"Talkin' about calves," said Ben Bowline as they were walking on in a body through the woods, "there was another adventure of mine which——"

"You're a liar!" suddenly interrupted a strident voice speaking in Spanish and then some bad language in the same tongue followed.

"Mah goodness, dat am fightin' talk!" exclaimed Bucephalus. "Ah wouldn' stan' dat, Sailorman."

"Jus' wait till I get my mudhooks onto him," growled Ben, "an' I'll let Trim know whether I'll stan' it or not."

"There are people on the island besides ourselves," muttered young Smith, getting close to Jack and Dick. "Maybe they own the calf."

"If you tell them anything about me," sputtered Billy, "I won't speak to you again in a week."

Then there was more talk in Spanish and Bucephalus put his hands over his ears and whistled.

"Mah wo'd! Ah done hear disreputable language in mah days, but nothin' to compaiah with that!" he declared emphatically. "It ain't respectable. Ef Ah meet de fellah wha' talk lak dat Ah's gwan to tell him wha' Ah done thought ob him."

There was still more of the talk, and Ben Bowline doubled his fists and said angrily:

"It's as bad to be told you're a liar in Spanish as it is in English or French or Dutch or any other lingo, an' I'm not goin' to take it from nobody. Just wait till I get hold — —"

Dick and Jack were both laughing heartily now, much to young Smith's amazement, Billy's surprise and the disgust of Ben Bowline, Bucephalus looking on and wondering what had come over his "young gentlemen" as he was accustomed to call them.

"What are you two fellows laughing at?" asked Billy.

"I don't see anything funny in it!" sputtered Ben.

"I think it's awful!" murmured Jesse W.

"Why, those are not men talking," laughed Dick.

"They aren't!" exclaimed Billy.

"Mebby dat am all imagination, sah!" added Bucephalus.

"What is it if it isn't men!" asked Ben.

"Parrots!" laughed Jack. "Don't you remember, you fellows, what we told you happened to us the other day when we were ashore together, Dick and I?"

"H'm! and I forgot all about it," chuckled Billy.

"Oh, that's different!" said J.W., greatly relieved.

"Parrots?" asked Ben. "Poll parrots? Well, I'll be keelhauled!"

"Mah we 'd! Ah knowed parrots could talk an' use de mos' obstreperous vocabulary at dat," declared the negro cook, "but Ah done suspected dat dey was men, fo' shuah Ah did."

The parrots, for such indeed they were, as all the party now realized, continued to talk and scream and chatter, and in a short time the boys and their companions caught sight of a number of them as they came out into a more open bit of woods.

"We were a bit alarmed ourselves, as you may remember," said Jack, "when we first heard them, and it was some little time before we realized that they were not men."

"They have caught the talk of men who have been to the island," added Percival, "and probably that of men who are here now. That calf is a tame creature and is probably owned by some one now on the island. The parrots may have heard them."

"If that is the sort of talk they heard, the birds were not in very good company," remarked Billy, "and it is just as well that we did not meet them this time. In fact, I hope we won't."

"Well, I'm glad it was only Poll parrots!" grunted Ben, "for I was ready for a fight."

"I'm glad myself," echoed Jesse W., greatly relieved, "for I don't want to get into a fight at all."

"That accounts for the milk in the cocoanut," laughed Billy. "I wondered what you two fellows were laughing at. If it had been Dick alone I would not have thought so much of it, but Jack has more sense."

"Thank you," said Dick dryly. "I know a tame calf from a wild bull, however, if I haven't much sense."

"Come ahead, boys," said Jack. "We must get back to the yacht. If there are other men on the island besides ourselves we do not want to meet them just now. They are not a desirable lot, most likely."

The entire party then pushed on, and in a short time reached the shore, got their boat and returned to the yacht.

CHAPTER XIII

A STRANGE LIGHT AT SEA

The captain and Dr. Wise were very much interested in the report that the boys brought back from their walk through the woods, and to the top of the hill in the interior of the island.

"If there are people here they know how to get out through the reefs," observed the principal, "for they must have come here once, and no doubt are in communication with the people outside."

"They may have lived here all their lives," returned the captain. "I never saw any one on these islands, natives, I mean, that knew very much. We can't tell how long they have lived here, they and their ancestors, of course, and these fellows probably don't know when they came, and don't suppose there is any other place in the world."

"H'm! that does not speak for a very high state of intelligence," remarked the doctor with a grunt.

"You won't find it in these natives nor even in the half breeds, sir," the captain returned. "The rating is pretty low. It'll be interesting to see these people, but I don't think that you will find them very intelligent. You'd better not expect too much."

The next day there was nothing to be seen of the wreck, and when Jack and Percival went to the wooded point to look for the place where they had descended when they first found it, there was nothing but a great hole into which the sea poured, and made a great disturbance at every tide.

"That's the last of that," said Jack. "No one would believe us if we told them we had gone down there and found a vessel fast in the rocks."

"But we know we did, for we have the evidences of it, and you are at least a couple of thousand dollars richer by it. That will help you a lot in getting your education, my boy, and give your mother something as well."

"Yes, and she is the first one to be considered," said Jack.

There had been no answers as yet to the captain's wireless messages, and that day he sent out another one, this time to the owners of the vessel in New York, addressing Mr. Smith in particular, thereby hoping to receive attention.

Meantime, the boys went on with recitations, wrote descriptions of the different parts of the island they had seen, took excursions on the bay and through the woods, and got up little entertainments to pass away the evenings so that altogether they were kept quite busy, and, as a consequence, were very well content with their situation, although it was not just what they had expected when they left home.

The day after sending out the personal message to Mr. Smith the captain of the yacht picked up a message which, although not addressed to him, was the first he had been able to pick up, and was of some interest on that account if on no other.

The message was to some government official in Florida, and related to a certain smuggler who had been defrauding the government by sending shipments of tobacco without paying the duty thereon.

"Are on track of Rollins and smuggler crew. Sighted them near Isle of Pines. Will keep on watch there and in Caribbean."

Such was the message and the captain, although not especially interested in Rollins, whoever he might be, was glad to get any information from the outside world which seemed so far away, although almost at their very doors.

He sent a wireless to the sender of the message, and asked if information of their situation could be sent to the government, and help despatched to them, hoping by this means to receive some recognition at last.

"If I get other folks' messages some one will probably get mine," said the captain, "and by communicating with these people I may finally get attention. Rollins? Don't remember to have heard of him. There's probably a gang of them working between our border, Cuba and the

South American ports. Whistling cyclones! they might be working among some of these little islands. A man who would defraud his government is no better than a pirate and pirates used to hang around these waters a lot. It isn't such an unlikely thing that these new pirates should do it now."

The next day quite unexpectedly the captain got a call and at once sent for the doctor and said:

"I've had word at last. From our owners. From Mr. Smith himself. He has just heard from us, and is going to send out a vessel to get us away from here. It seems that one of our smaller vessels, a steamer, has been captured by some smugglers working around Cuba, Porto Rico and the neighborhood, who are using it in their trade. Some of the men got away, and took the news to Havana. The name of the vessel is a good deal like our own, and Smith thought that we had been taken at first, and began a lot of investigating. Then he got our messages, which had been held up by some one else, thinking they were fakes, or some boys' play. These young wireless operators make a lot of trouble now and then."

"Well, as long as we know that help is being sent to us we can feel relieved," said the doctor. "That is something, at any rate, but — —"

"But you don't think that it will do any good, Doctor?"

"Well, if you cannot get out how is any one else going to get in?" the doctor asked, as if merely seeking for information, and not being especially interested in the matter.

"There's something in that, sir," replied Captain Storms musingly, "but we'll see how it turns out when they get here. At any rate we are not forgotten altogether, and that is something."

The boys were told about the message, and were greatly interested, Jesse W. saying to Jack:

"Now I'll have a chance to speak to father about you, Jack, and to tell him what you have done for me. He has always been interested in you, and now he will be all the more so."

"Never mind doing too much for me, J.W., or you will spoil me altogether," laughed Jack, who, nevertheless, felt grateful to the younger boy for his interest. "We Hilltop boys should help each other, and so I don't deserve any extra credit for simply doing what is expected of me. It is only the big brother idea which is gaining ground every day, and is a good thing both for the little brothers and the big ones."

That night as Jack Sheldon lay asleep in his berth in the cabin set off for the Hilltop boys, he was suddenly awakened by a bright light flashing in his face, there being a porthole opposite.

"That's odd!" he murmured, as he sat up and looked around. "Where does that light come from? Or did I only imagine it?"

At that moment the light flashed in his face again, and he got out of his berth and went over to the porthole, looking out to see where the light could have come from, there being only water on that side.

The yacht had changed her position, and was now in sight of the outer bay, and having changed the direction of her head on account of the tide, the boy could now look out upon the bay, which he had not been able to do at the time he went to bed.

He saw the flash again, and in a moment realized that some one out there, probably beyond the reefs, was using a regular code of signals, a thing he had himself done with his pocket electric light.

Having had this experience he was familiar with the code, and at once began to read the message sent by those outside, whoever they might be.

"That cannot be the steamer Mr. Smith has sent," he mused. "No, of course not. 'Where are you? Am dodging government vessel.' Why, that must be one of the smugglers that the captain told us about. But where is the man he is signaling? I wish I could tell that."

The signals ceased, but presently the lights flashed again, and Jack read the message:

"Why don't you answer? Am waiting."

"My word! I believe the fellow takes our lights for the smuggler's, and thinks that he is in here. It would be just the place for him. By Jove! I have a mind to answer him myself, and get him in here. Then we could get out. Even if a smuggler takes us out that is better than waiting."

His pocket flash was in a convenient place, and he quickly got it out and flashed out through the port:

"In the bay. Come inside."

After sending this message he waited a few minutes, and then saw the reply being flashed to him:

"Cannot. Don't know the passage. Come out"

"H'm! that's too bad," muttered Jack. "I was in hope I could get him in here. I'd like to know—I guess I'd better see the captain."

Partly dressing himself he hurried on deck, and looked for the light, but could see nothing.

An anchor watch was kept, or supposed to be at least, but Jack saw the man on deck fast asleep on a bench against the house on deck instead of keeping a lookout as he was supposed to do.

He could not see any vessel's light out at sea, and saw no more flashes, although he looked for them for several minutes.

"Well, I can't go to waking the captain in the middle of the night," he said, "and it is likely this fellow has gone. It is simply another disappointment. I think I'll go to bed."

CHAPTER XIV

THE MAN WITH THE WHITE MUSTACHE

In the morning Jack told the captain, Dr. Wise, and a few of his most intimate friends among the boys under the promise of keeping it quiet, the strange event of the previous night, asking the doctor if he had done right in not calling the captain.

"If you had aroused me I would probably have been mad," chuckled the captain, "and could not have done anything anyhow. It is clear that there is a way in here, although we don't know it, and that this fellow you saw signaling mistook our lights for those of one of his evil associates. I'd like to watch him, but there is no use in crying over spilled milk, and you did all right in not calling me."

"It is all very singular," said the doctor, knitting his brows. "Of course we would like to get out of here, but as to seeking the assistance of a smuggler— —"

"I'd as soon go out under his escort as that of any one else," laughed Storms, "although we might get in trouble afterward if a government vessel happened to see us in company with smugglers. Well, I guess it won't be long now before the relief steamer comes, but— —"

"But they may not know the way in, and we are as badly off as before," finished the doctor. "I don't see that we have advanced any, except, perhaps, to let people know where we are."

"And you think there is little satisfaction in that?" with a grin. "We might be worse off, however, so I guess we had better wait and trust to good luck. Clever game, that of Jack's, wasn't it, stealing the fellow's despatches?"

"Why, yes, clever in a way," admitted the doctor, glaring at the captain through his big black-rimmed glasses, "but does it not savor somewhat of—h'm—of deception? Pretending to be one person when he was another, and quite a different one, by the way?"

"But he did not pretend to be anybody. He simply flashed a message, and if that fellow outside took him for another person it was not Mr. Sheldon's fault. All is fair in love and war, you know."

"H'm! so I have heard, but as I have been in neither I cannot say whether it is so or not. However, I am not accusing you, Sheldon, you understand? I suppose, under the circumstances, that what you did was perfectly justifiable. At any rate, we shall not have to wait for this person to come and take us out. But where was the person to whom he was sending signals? You did not see him, Captain?"

"No, indeed, and I wonder that my man on deck did not see them. Asleep, I'll warrant. That means loss of shore liberty to him for some time. The other fellow was not here, of course. How could he get in?"

"I believe there is a way, sir," spoke up Jack, "and that this place is used as a retreat for smugglers. If not just here, then some part of the island. How about the calf we saw? I thought at the time that there were people here, but did not think of smugglers."

"Why, I guess you've been reading about Captain Kidd and Blackbeard and those old pirates, and have got your head full of secret lairs and all that sort of stuff."

"Oh, no," smiled Jack in reply, "but evil men hide in woods and mountains and all sorts of odd places as much now as they did in the old days. There is just as much of this in modern times as there was in the old, but it is accompanied with greater danger."

"Yes, I reckon it is. At any rate, I'd like to get hold of these rascals. There'll be a pretty big reward for them, I fancy."

The boys left the cabin and during the afternoon Jack, Dick and young Smith set out for a stroll over the island, taking one of the paths already made, so as not to subject the younger boy to too much trouble.

"I hardly think these smugglers are on the island," said Jack, as they walked on, "or, at least, I don't think that they got in through the reefs. They could have landed on the other side, although there are many difficulties connected with it, not to say dangers. You remember the rocks, Dick? And there is a good deal of surf there also. One would need to be careful in making it. A vessel could lie to, of course, while boats landed the men, and that has probably been done."

"Yes, I suppose so," said Percival carelessly, thinking of other things at the moment, and not paying much attention.

The boys walked on without paying much attention to where they were going, young Smith being greatly pleased at being with the older boys, but at length Jack stopped, looked around him, and said with the least bit of alarm in his tone:

"H'm! I believe we are where Billy was treed by the calf the other day or pretty near it, at any rate. We thought there might be people in the neighborhood, but we did not see them."

"I suppose it might be as well to go back," said Percival. "It would not be pleasant to run across a lot of half-civilized natives to say nothing of smugglers."

"No, it would not," and at that instant there was a rustling in the bushes not far away, and two men stepped out, the singular appearance of one of them causing Jack to turn suddenly pale.

This man was of good height and build and evidently quite strong, and was, besides, a person of superior intellect if not of the best tendencies, as his face indicated, but what attracted most attention was the fact that while his mustache was snowy white his hair and eyebrows were quite dark, this making him noticeable in a moment.

"You here, George——"

"Rollins," said the other, evidently thinking that Jack was about to pronounce another name, which was the fact. "Yes, I am here. It is safer than back in New York state or any of the states, in fact. May I ask what you are doing in this part of the world! I am as much surprised to see you here as you are to see me," and the man made a sudden quick signal with his left hand.

The Hilltop Boys on Lost Island

Jack heard a rustle behind him, and turned quickly, but not soon enough to escape the quick rush of three big, strong, bearded men who sprang upon him and his companions and held them fast.

"What does this mean, George—Rollins?" asked Jack, hesitating at pronouncing the name, "Who are these men!"

"Friends of mine," laughed the man with the white mustache. "Business partners I might say."

"The majority of your business partners get in jail or are shot by the police, Mr. Rollins," said Jack. "Are these the same sort? What business are you in now?" and then a look of intelligence shot across the boy's face, as he remembered that Rollins was the name of the smuggler he had but recently heard mentioned.

The other saw this look, and said with an evil glance:

"I think you have heard the name before. What are you doing here? You are in the government service, you and your boy friends? What is this uniform you wear?"

"That of the students of the Hilltop Academy. You knew that I was one of them, for on the occasion of our last meeting——"

"I say, Jack," said Percival suddenly, "this is the man who was concerned in the robbery of the Riverton Bank, your——" and the boy suddenly paused, a deep flush on his face.

"His father, you were going to say," laughed the other, an evil look crossing his countenance. "Yes, you are quite right, I am——"

"You are not!" cried Jack hotly. "You married my mother a year or so after my own father's death, and made her life miserable, but that does not make you my father, and you well know that I have never admitted your claim. No court would admit it. Courts? You take good care to keep away from all of them, Mr. Rollins, as you choose to call yourself."

"Take them away," said the man with the white mustache. "Let no harm come to them. I don't understand why they are on the island, but it would be awkward if any of their friends should know of our presence here. Don't let them get away, but don't hurt them."

The men were much stronger than the boys, and Jack saw the futility of a struggle during which the younger boy might be hurt, and he, therefore, submitted to being led away, hoping to escape at some later time.

The boys were led some little distance to a little opening where they saw a number of small crudely built houses, several dark-skinned men, who were neither Indians nor negroes, but perhaps a combination of both, and a number of domesticated animals, calves, pigs, a sheep and several fowls.

There were people on the island, therefore, as they had supposed, and these men visited the place on occasion as in the present instance.

There was a strongly built house somewhat larger than the rest on one side of the little village, and here the three boys were taken and locked in a small square room with one window, this being small and protected with an iron bar, evidently to make it safer, Jack noticing several cases in one corner opposite the window.

"Make yourselves comfortable, young gentlemen," laughed Rollins, as he called himself. "You will be set free, but not at present," and with that he went away, and the door was stoutly locked.

CHAPTER XV

JESSE W. IS SENT FOR HELP

All was quiet in a few minutes after the man with the white mustache had left the boys in the room with the barred windows, and presently Percival said, half apologetically, but with the greatest kindness:

"You know I did not mean to call that man any relation of yours, Jack, but the sudden recollection of the last time you met him when I did not see him at all made me blurt out suddenly. I did stop, though."

Jack had come unexpectedly upon his stepfather during his first term at the Academy, several months previous, the man at that time being concerned in the robbery of a bank near the Academy, but escaping capture and suddenly disappearing, Jack had hoped, forever.

He felt nervous and discouraged now that the man had again come into his life, and he sat in a corner of the room on a chest and thought deeply, Percival presently saying to him in cheery tones:

"Brace up, Jack. It is not like you to give way to despondency. What are we going to do? We can't stay here even if that fellow with the white mustache has given orders that we are not to be harmed."

"I tell you what," whispered young Smith. "That window is small, but not too small to put me through. You have done that before, you know. If you can get that bar loose it will be easy enough to put me out, and then I will go straight to the vessel and get the captain, old Ben Bowline, and a lot of sailors to come and get you out."

"You know the way, do you, Jesse W., you won't get lost!" asked Percival, catching at the idea. "You are a plucky little fellow, but I don't want you to take any risks."

"They are nothing but what I can take easy enough," answered the other quickly. "Don't you suppose I would do anything for Jack?

And for you, too. You have both done a lot for me, and this isn't much. You get me through the window, and I'll do the rest."

Jack arose quietly, crossed the room, took hold of the iron bar put across the window and tested it.

"I believe we could pull it loose, Dick," he said in a low tone, not knowing if there were any one outside who might hear him. "It is only driven into the frame, and I believe we could pull out frame and all."

"Let me look at it," said Percival, and, taking hold of the bar, he suddenly swelled up his muscles, gave it a quick, sharp wrench, and had it out with a part of the frame as well.

"H'h! great protection that was!" he laughed. "I suppose they thought the window was too small for any one to get through, and it is for most folks, but Jesse W. is only half size and we can put him through all right."

"And I'll put through the other part," said the younger boy. "I am glad I can do something for you two, for you have both of you done a lot for me at one time or another."

"But see here, J.W., do you understand that there is considerable danger in getting away?" asked Jack in a serious tone. "These fellows may be watching, and they would handle you roughly if they caught you. And then it is dark going through the woods, for the moon does not rise till pretty late, and you might fall down some——"

"And I might not!" interrupted the other in a decided tone. "I have a pocket light with me. I always carry one now, whether I think I am going to need it or not, and I can find my way easy enough. Besides, I have a pocket compass as well, and I know which way the vessel lies, and I am going to get you boys out of here and that's all there is to it!"

"All right!" and Jack smiled at the smaller boy's determination. "But I wouldn't let you go if I didn't think you had the pluck to carry it out, and that the only difficulties are at the outset. Listen at the door,

Dick, and I'll see how the land lies in this direction," and Jack pulled the chest to the window and looked out.

He could not see very far, but he saw that there were no huts on that side, and that it was not far to the woods, and calculated that the boy could get to them without being observed.

"All right, J.W., the coast is clear," he said. "You are sure you know the way and the general direction? What is it, in fact?"

"About south, and I will get in sight of the water as soon as I can. It will not be dark for some little time yet, and I ought to get to the yacht before sunset or a little after at any rate."

"Very good. Keep in the open as much as you can after you get away from here, and don't run too fast."

"All right. Are you ready?" and the boy stood on the chest beside Jack, looking up into the latter's face with such an air of determination that he laughed and said:

"Yes, I'm ready, up with you!" and Jack lifted the little fellow to the window level, and put him through, Percival saying in a low tone:

"It's all right. I don't hear a sound. I imagine they are all away somewhere, for I can neither see nor hear anything."

"Out you go!" said Jack, dropping the boy to the ground, and looking out to see that he was all right. "Now then, cut!"

He watched the boy till he disappeared in the woods, and then as he neither saw any one nor heard anything of an alarming nature, he said in a tone of great relief:

"He is all right, and I believe he will get there without trouble. I had an idea he would, or I would not have let him go."

"There he is, only half a boy, you might say," said Percival, "but ready to undertake anything for us, no matter how dangerous and there are those big overgrown bullies, Herring and Merritt, who would go all to bits if they had the half of this to do. I tell you, Jesse

W. Smith is worth both of them in a lump, and with considerable on his side of the ledger after that, Jack."

"Yes, so he is," agreed Jack.

"And now we will simply have to wait, I suppose?"

"I don't see anything else. The window is too small for us and the door seems to be very strong and heavy, and securely locked. No, I considered these points before I let the boy go."

"But suppose our man with the white mustache should return and miss him?" asked Percival.

"Well, we will put the bar back in its place, put the chest in the corner, and place our coats in a neat pile over there where it is darkest. There are things that we can put under them, and there is the boy fast asleep after his tramp through the woods."

"A good idea, Jack! You are full of resources. Now I would never have thought of a way out of the trouble, but only of the trouble itself."

They replaced the bar so that no one would know by a casual glance that it had been tampered with, put the chest back where they had taken it from, and, gathering up a few loose articles from the floor, made a bundle of them and spread their coats over it.

"A mere reference to the boy being asleep will be enough," said Jack. "The look of the thing is enough to carry out the idea, and they will accept it without question."

"To be sure, and in the meantime the plucky young fellow is hustling to get back to the vessel and bring us help."

Having settled all this the boys sat down and waited, now and then conversing, and occasionally listening for any sound that would denote the return of the so-called Rollins and the men with him.

It was getting on toward sunset when Jack heard Rollins and another man talking outside, although he could not see them when he went to the little window and looked out.

"You say there is a vessel in the bay?"

"Yes, inside the reefs."

"Government vessel?"

"No, private yacht, the one these boys belong on. It's a school on a vacation or tour or something."

"Do they know the way through the reefs!"

"I guess not. They were washed in the other night when there was a cyclone or tidal wave."

"They did not come here after us?"

"No, they didn't know anything about us. They have been here for some time, a week I guess, and can't get out."

"H'm! let them stay here then!" growled the man with the white mustache. "They can't bother us any. If they don't know the way out, which very few do, they'll have to stay here for all I can see."

"But suppose we want to get in on that side ourselves?"

"They could not make us any trouble. We don't want to get in there at this time, although it is a better hiding place than this."

"Then you're going to let them stay there?"

"Certainly. They can't do us any harm. After we get away with our cargo we don't care what happens to them."

The men went away or stopped talking, at any rate, and Jack did not hear any further conversation between them.

"They will probably let us out as soon as they are ready to go," he said to Percival, "but we don't want to stay here till they get ready to let us out, and then there is just a chance that they may forget us altogether. It was just as well that we sent Jesse W. off on his errand."

"I think so myself, and I don't doubt that he will carry it out."

"If Rollins knows the way out through the reefs," said Jack presently, "we might either force or persuade him to pilot us out. If we should capture him we might force him to do it. Otherwise, I might persuade him to do it on consideration of allowing him to escape after we were perfectly safe outside. Very few know of the way out, and it is not likely that the vessel which they are sending to our relief will have any good pilot for these waters on board."

"You don't know positively that this man knows the passage!"

"No, I do not, but he does know some one who does, to judge by his talk, and if he cannot be bargained with perhaps the other man can. I am averse to having anything to do with the man, as you can readily understand, but I do not want to see the whole Hilltop Academy kept prisoners here for an indefinite time."

When it began to grow dark one of the men who had brought them to the place came in with some food and a bottle of wine, and said, as he put it on a chest:

"There's something for you to eat. Other boy asleep, h'm? Well, there is all the more for you then."

Then the man went away, never noticing the little bit of deception which the boys had practised, locking the door after him.

"The things to eat are all right," said Jack, after the man had gone, "but we would better not touch the wine. I never do, anyhow. This is likely to be drugged to make us sleep, so that we will give no trouble."

"I don't want it anyhow," said Dick.

The boys ate a supper, and then, as it grew dark, sat and waited for some sign of their friends, and at last when it was quite dark hearing a peculiar whistle somewhere outside.

"That's the Hilltop signal!" whispered Percival "Aid is at hand!"

CHAPTER XVI

BEN'S STRANGE STORY

Jack jumped upon the chest, which he quickly dragged to the little window, and answered the signal, one generally used by the Hilltop boys when they wished to communicate with each other at a distance.

In a moment it was answered, and then young Smith ran up under the window, and said eagerly:

"You are all right, boys, you are there still, and safe!"

"Yes," answered Jack. "Who is there?"

"Some of the boys, Ben Bowline, the captain and Buck, all ready for a fight if necessary."

"All right. I don't think you will need to make one."

Percival was at the door now, and in a moment he heard the outer one fall in with a crash, and then came the rush of many feet.

There were shouts outside, but these were drowned by the yells of the boys, and of the old sailor.

"Are yo' dere, sah?" the boys heard Bucephalus say in a few moments, just outside the door.

"Yes, but we are locked in."

"Nevah min' dat, jus' lemme get mah head at it an' Ah'll break it down in a hurry, sah."

"Here, stop that!" roared Ben Bowline. "You'll crack yer skull!"

"No, sah, Ah's used to dem things!" guffawed Bucephalus.

"Don't you know that his name means 'ox-headed,' Ben?" cried Percival with a laugh. "Why, he could split a two-inch plank with that head of his. Let him do it, but first wait till I get out of the way."

It was not necessary for Bucephalus to butt the door down, however, as one of the men with Rollins had been captured, and was forced to open the door with his key.

It was the same man who had brought them food and wine, and at the sight of the boys, for lights had been brought, he exclaimed:

"Guess you boys didn't drink anything?"

"No, we did not," said Percival. "Won't you have it your self?"

"Huh! I think not. But where's the little fellow? The one that was asleep when I come in."

"Here I am!" piped up Jesse W. himself, "and you'll find that I am pretty wide awake."

The boys picked up their coats, and put them on, and the man muttered, his eyes opening wider every moment:

"Huh! that was a neat trick! Then the boy was not there at all?"

"No, he was on his way for help," said Jack. "Never judge too much by appearances. Still, I am glad you did this time."

The boys and their friends now left the house, the man being taken a short distance to prevent his giving the alarm, although the natives had already scattered in many directions at the coming of Ben, Buck and the boys.

"Young Smith got to us all right," said Harry to Jack and Dick, "and we set out without delay. You must have had quite an adventure."

"So we did, and it might have been worse. Rollins is on this part of the island, sir," to the captain. "He got in yesterday or to-day, I am not sure which. I do not believe he has seen the man who was signaling to him last night, and I do not think he knows anything about him. He does know that government vessels are on the watch for him, however, and I think he will shortly get away from here."

"I wish we could get word to them so as to stop him," growled the captain. "These smugglers give honest traders a bad reputation, for folks think we are all alike."

A considerable number of the Hilltop boys had come to the rescue of the two boys, and these were now carried on the shoulders of the others, and a triumphal march back to the vessel was begun, young Smith being taken up as well as Jack and Dick, the boys saying that he had traveled enough for one day and that he needed a rest.

Many of the boys had pocket lights with them, and others cut pine branches and made torches of them so that there was light enough to show them the way, and it was not necessary to wait for the moon to rise.

The boys sang and shouted, and made a lot of noise on the way back so that if the smugglers or any of the natives had had any idea of attacking them they would have been deterred by the very din.

They reached the shore at length, and were taken on board the yacht, Bucephalus presently announcing that supper was ready, the boys having the best of appetites for it, and making it a feast in honor of Jack, Dick and young Jesse W., who was considered as much a hero as his older schoolmates, and was certainly regarded so by them.

Not all the boys had gone over to the other side, some staying away on account of the fatigue of the journey and others, noticeably Herring and his cronies, because they were either not asked or would not have gone if they had been.

It was a feast in honor of the three boys, nevertheless, and those who were not ready to join in praise of the heroes were wise enough to keep quiet and not to make any dissent.

After supper Jack and a few of the boys discussed the situation, and tried to calculate how long it would take the vessel which Mr. Smith had sent out to reach them.

"If we knew that, we would know how long we would have to wait," observed Arthur. "Some vessels are faster than others."

"It would take at least three or four days," said Jack, "and if he has sent a fast vessel and given directions to make all speed they might be here in less time. Then they must pick up a pilot who would be likely to know these seas, and who is used to making difficult passages. Any ordinary pilot would not do. He should have a special one."

"And he cannot tell just what is required till he gets here, and, perhaps, would have to hunt one up, and there is more lost time," said Harry dolefully. "It's a pity we are wasting so much time."

"Yes, but I don't see how we are going to help ourselves."

"No, perhaps not."

Late that night Jack was awakened as he lay asleep in his berth, not by a flash, as before, but by hearing some one say, as he went by the door:

"It can't be, it's too much like the flying Dutchman."

"That's what I say, but all the same I was sure I saw one come in through the reefs."

"You didn't see any lights?"

"No, but I could make out her masts and rigging."

The two men went on, and Jack heard no more.

"There has some vessel come in through the reefs," he said to himself as he sat up in bed. "I must try to find them to-morrow. I have always said that I thought it possible for a vessel to get through if one knew the passage, and this shows that it has been done. No wonder these men thought it was a phantom ship."

Partially dressing himself he went on deck, and looked around him.

He could see nothing, and he hardly expected to do so, but had yielded to impulse and had come on deck.

Ben Bowline presently came up, looked at him, touched his grizzled forelock, and said:

"Sir to you. Come up to get the air?"

"Yes," Jack answered shortly.

"Kind of a pretty night, don't you think, sir!" the old sailor said after a pause during which he stood balancing himself first on one foot and then on the other.

"Yes, it is a fine starlight night. The moon ought to be coming up soon, and then we can see things better."

"Yes, so we can. Was you looking for anything particular, sir?" in a mysterious tone.

"How about that vessel, Ben?" asked Jack in a low tone. "Are you sure you saw her? What was she, the long, low, rakish craft we read of in old stories or a saucy steam yacht with tremendous speed?"

"Sh! the old man might hear us," cautioned Ben Bowline. "Do you know I don't want to think it were the Flying Dutchman 'cause it's plumb bad luck to see her, but how is a live ship going to get in here?"

"Easy enough, if she knows the way, Ben. Don't say anything about it, but are you sure you saw something?"

"Well, I dunno, but I think I did. She was out yonder, just where you can see the open water, and she was only there half a jiffy, as you might say. Tom saw her, too, or I would have thought I was dreaming."

"Steamer, Ben?" asked Jack, sure now that there was something in the old fellow's story.

"Reckon she was, though I did see something white, which gave me a creepy feeling like as if I'd seen a apparition or something similar. Maybe she had sail on to help her steam. Some of 'em do."

"And you saw her for a short time only!"

"Yes, sir, not half a minute nor half that even. There wasn't time to say 'Jack Robinson' twice, sir, before she was out of sight."

"Well, if she came in she can get out, and so can we, Ben. Keep this quiet till I speak to the captain about it. It will be just as well not to have every one know it, and have it talked about all over the vessel."

"Shouldn't wonder if it would, sir," and as Jack walked away the old sailor continued his own passage up and down the deck.

"There are probably places to hide that we have not seen," thought the boy, as he took a turn of the deck, and then started to go below, "and we may not be able to see this vessel in the morning. I shall have a look for her, nevertheless. If there is to be a bargain made and I don't see why there should not be, unless we trade directly with lawbreakers and assist them. That we could not do, of course, but if we hire a pilot we are not supposed to know whether he is honest or not."

The question was a puzzling one, and Jack had not solved it when he went below, turned in and quickly fell asleep.

In the morning, nothing having been seen of any strange vessel from the deck of the yacht, Jack told Percival quietly what he had heard, and after breakfast they went ashore and set out for a search for the stranger.

"If she is here," Jack said, "she is one of the smugglers, and will not want to be seen. If we can find her it may mean that we can get out of our strange prison."

"How are we going to find her, Jack? There are probably plenty of hiding places about here that we don't dream of."

"I know it, Dick, but we must find them if we want to leave here. I do not think that Smith will be able to get us out, and if we can do it ourselves, so much the better."

"Yes, and all the more credit to us, Jack."

CHAPTER XVII

DISCOVERIES AND DISAPPOINTMENTS

The boys landed at the point where they had first gone ashore, well up in the bay, as that would give them less walking, and pushed toward the north, keeping as near to the shore as they could in the hope of being thus better able to see the hidden smuggler in case she was still at the island.

Making their way over rough ground, they at length came to an opening in the rocks which was quite high enough for them to enter, and Jack said in an eager tone:

"It is possible we may find something here, Dick. This seems to be a cave, and smugglers and men of that sort make such places convenient."

"It looks rather dark, Jack," murmured Percival. "We had a pretty gruesome experience in a dark cave when we first came to the island and I don't want to repeat it."

"You won't find any devil fish in there, Dick," said Jack reassuringly. "Besides, we have our flashes with us and are armed as well, and if we do find anything uncanny we can put up a good fight, I imagine."

"That's all right, Jack, but once I have an experience of that sort I am a little shy at venturing into a place anything like it. The mere look of this cave made me think of the other."

"But there is no water here and it may be only a hole in the rocks after all. Then it may lead to some retreat of these smuggler folk, and if it does, so much the better."

"All right, Jack, I am with you," said Percival, and the boys entered the hole in the rocks, as Jack called it.

It was more than that, as they presently discovered, for they found that it extended much farther than they thought, and Jack, turning on his pocket flash when there began to be less and less light to guide them, saw that the passage went on for some distance.

It was high enough for them to walk upright and wide enough for three or four persons to walk abreast, there being a few turns, but none sharp enough to cut off the view ahead for some distance.

"Well, we won't get under water as we did in the other place, Jack," observed Percival as they walked on, meeting the first sharp turn and being now unable to see behind them, "for we are going toward the interior of the island and not toward the sea."

"No, and there will be no one to tumble down rocks upon us and shut us in, or think they did, as happened before. In fact, the place seems to be decidedly uninteresting, Dick."

"Nothing has happened so far, if that is what you mean," laughed the other, "but you never can tell."

They made one or two more sharp turns and at length came to an opening of greater magnitude where they could see three or four passages leading in different directions, some very narrow and one wide enough for them to walk side by side.

"Which one shall we take, Jack?" asked Percival. "The place begins to grow interesting now that we have several routes to choose from. Does it look as if men had been here? Do you see any smudges on the walls or any footprints in the dust? Is this just an accident, or has it been cut out and made of use for a hiding place?"

"No, there are no smudges which might have been made by torches, Dick, and I don't see any footprints except our own. I don't believe any one has been in here for years."

"Then you think that there may have been some one here at some time, Jack? It has been used?"

"Yes, for it has not the looks of a natural cavern which has not yet been discovered. It has been cleaned up to a certain extent. Still, I do not think that the particular gang of malefactors we are looking for has ever occupied it."

"Then there is not much use in our going any farther, Jack?"

"No, not if we want to find Rollins and the rest."

"Suppose we take the widest passage, Jack!"

"Very well. Come ahead."

They went on for twenty feet, when the floor of the passage began to take a sudden decline which increased at every step.

"Hold on, Dick," said Jack, holding his light low and flashing it along the rough floor. "This thing may take a sudden drop and——"

"So it does!" gasped Percival, lying at full length on the floor and crawling carefully forward a pace or two. "It takes a drop for fair. It is a lucky thing you noticed it."

"Then we may as well go back, for I don't care to take a drop I don't know how deep."

"I'll see," muttered Percival, picking up a loose stone as big as his fist and tossing it ahead of him.

Not until several seconds had passed did the boys hear the sound of the stone falling into water, and Percival said with a sigh of relief:

"Well, we didn't go that way, at any rate. Come on, Jack, there is nothing to be seen in that direction."

The boys returned to the place where the passages diverged, and Percival suggested that they take one of the narrower paths and follow it for a time.

"All right," laughed Jack, "but I don't believe we shall find any more than we have already found. In fact, I don't believe the smugglers know of this place at all and we won't find out anything."

However, they proceeded down the narrow path till they suddenly found themselves at the end, where the place widened into a chamber about ten feet square, and here they saw a sight which made Percival tremble.

It was a pile of human skeletons reaching nearly to the roof of the vault and thrown promiscuously about like so much rubbish.

"I say, I've got enough of this!" gasped the young fellow. "Let's get out of this, Jack, before we find anything worse. First the bottomless pit and then a charnel house. I am satisfied!"

"It is not a very pleasant sight," said Jack musingly, "but they cannot do us any harm. They have probably been here for years."

The boys returned to the chamber they had left and then went back along the way they had come without seeking to explore any other passages.

Getting out into the light at last, they proceeded with their search for the smugglers, resolving not to enter any more mysterious caves, but to look for places where a vessel might be able to hide.

"There must be a lot of coves along here," said Jack, "that we have not been able to find on account of the difficulty of making one's way along the rocks, but now we are looking for them we don't mind doing a lot of scrambling."

"No, we are used to that, and, besides, we are alone, and haven't young Smith with us. I suppose he would have been delighted to come, for he likes being with us, but it would have been too much of a task for him."

"And yet he would not have complained, Dick. He is a plucky little chap. Just think of his going into the cabin of the wreck, up to his knees in the water, to get that bag of gold just because he said he would."

"Yes, it was a nervy thing to do, and there are bigger boys in the Academy who would not have done it. But I say, Jack, it is getting pretty rough along here. I am afraid we may have to change our route."

They had come upon a mass of high rocks over which it was well nigh impossible to make their way, and Jack stopped, looked around him and said:

"It seems a pretty tough job, Dick. Suppose you give me a boost, however, and let me see if I can get to the top of this one. I am lighter than you, and perhaps I can make it."

"All right, Jack, just as you say," and Dick bent his back so that his companion could get upon his shoulders, and then straightened up slowly, Jack holding on by some of the projections in the rock and going up with him, being able to reach a bit higher when Percival was at his full height and saying, with some satisfaction:

"That is fine, Dick. I should reach the top now. Catch me if I come tumbling down, however."

"I don't think you will, Jack. You are a regular cat to keep your feet, and I guess you are all right."

Clinging with toes and fingers to the rock and going up inch by inch, Jack at length reached a point whence it was easier climbing, and here he advanced more rapidly than before, Percival watching him closely, and standing ready to catch him in case he happened to lose his footing.

Jack did not, however, and at last, as he reached the top of the rock, threw himself forward and found himself on a flat, but somewhat rough surface a few yards in extent with higher rocks on one side, but nothing in front of him.

Beyond, at some little distance, there were other rocks, but he judged that if he went to the edge of the rock to which he had climbed he might see something, and he, therefore, crept along cautiously for fear of being seen, until he reached the edge.

Here he looked over and saw that there was water below him, quite a good sized cove, in fact, which ran up from the shore to a considerable distance, apparently, but had a turn a few rods farther up in shore.

Looking the other way Jack could see the bay in which they lay, and said to himself:

"That is the way they could come, but now let us see if they did, and if there is room beyond for a vessel of any size to pass."

The higher mass of rock on his left prevented his going much farther, however, and he was thinking that he might be obliged to climb to the top of this, being unable to get around it, when he heard a suspicious sound below him, and lay flat on his face, peering cautiously over the edge.

There were some bushes and coarse grass here and these hid him somewhat from observation, while they did not prevent his seeing anything going on below.

The sound he had heard was the splash of oars and the hum of voices, and in a few moments he saw a boat containing two men appear around a corner of the higher rock, which descended sheer to the water's edge, and make its way slowly toward the open bay.

"I tell you there is one, Davis," Jack heard one of the men say, recognizing the voice as that of the man with the white mustache, as he always thought of him, and not as his stepfather.

In fact, he had long since repudiated any relationship whatever with the man, and regarded him as a stranger who had come into his life without any wish of his own, and whom he would willingly put out of it, and be satisfied never to see or hear of again.

"But weren't you in here the other night when I signaled?" asked the other man, who was rowing. "You answered and told me to come in."

"Me?" with a laugh. "I tell you I was not. I don't know the way in any more than you, though I know that there is one."

"But I saw lights, and I got flashes from some one on deck, in the regular code, too."

"They were from the deck of this yacht I told you of, and I will show her to you if you are patient. Go easy, though, for we may come in sight of her at any moment."

"But how about the signals I got? How could any one know I was out there, and how would they know the code?"

"They got you by accident, perhaps, and then were smart enough to take your signals and answer them. I know a boy who is clever enough for that. He is on the yacht, too. She has a lot of schoolboys who are on a trip to these seas. They were carried in here by a tidal wave, and now cannot get out, not knowing the passage."

"Well, I don't know it myself, and I never would have come in only for finding a pilot who knows the ins and outs of all the islands in the Caribbean, but if I noticed any lights when I came in I must have thought they were yours."

The men rowed on out of sight, for Jack did not care to lean over too far, partly from fear of falling and partly because he might be seen if any one else should happen to pass that way.

There had a vessel come into the bay, then, and she was now probably up the cove out of sight, and the man in the boat with the other was her captain.

"That is the man whose vessel I signaled the other night," thought Jack. "Rollins must have come over to this side and met him. They know each other, it seems. Birds of a feather flock together."

Not caring to expose himself to the risk of being seen by the men when they returned, Jack now crept back to the other side of the rock and began to descend carefully, Percival being at length able to help him.

"Well, Jack," said the latter when his friend was safe on the ground, "did you discover anything!"

"Yes, I did," and Jack told him briefly what he had seen and heard.

"H'm! then there was a vessel coming in last night, and old Ben was not mistaken?" exclaimed Percival.

"No, he was not, and she is in a cove somewhere on the other side of the rocks. I don't know how far up it goes, but there is one there. I could not see the vessel either."

"We must try to find it, Jack."

"Yes, and we must get around these rocks. There is no way of getting to the cove this way, unless we climb another high rock, and it is dangerous and we might be seen also."

"Then let's look for another way."

They went back for a distance, and then began clambering over masses of other rocks they came to, getting higher and higher, but at last coming to a great mass of ledge rock, which rose sheer above their heads for twenty feet without a single projection upon which they could rest their feet and without a crevice where they might get a finger hold.

"There is no use trying to get up there, Jack," murmured Percival in disgust. "A goat could not climb up there. Nothing without wings could manage it, in fact."

"No, there is clearly no getting around this way, Dick. We shall have to go back and try some other place. There is a vessel on the other side of those rocks, but how to get a sight of her is the question. I think we would better try to find the head of the cove."

They went back, therefore, to where they had tried to ascend the rocks, and pushed on toward the interior of the island, finding the way difficult, but at length getting clear of the rocks and after struggling through a perfect jungle coming out upon one of the paths they had themselves made in their explorations.

"Well, we know where we are now!" exclaimed Percival with considerable satisfaction, "but we seem to be no nearer the head of the cove than before. What are you going to do, Jack?"

"Look for the cove," said Jack tersely.

"All right, my boy, I am with you," said Dick with a chuckle, as if the idea was a most amusing one.

"Seems funny, doesn't it?" said Jack, smiling. "Well, we have had a lot of trouble, I admit, but you are not the one to give up when you undertake a task, and you know that I do not like to."

"Not only that you don't like to, Jack, but that you don't do it."

They set out toward the shore again, determined to find the cove if it were a possible thing, and looking for every possible clue to its whereabouts, and plunging into what seemed the most impassable thickets in their efforts, halting at nothing, in fact.

"We should have brought axes, Jack," muttered Percival in disgust, as both boys paused at length, tired and hot in a little glade where the way was clearer than before, and yet having no assurance that they were anywhere near the place they sought.

"Yes, but that is just like a couple of boys who are bound to do a thing and don't make all their calculations ahead. Our hind thought is better than our forethought, Dick."

"Yes, but we could not think of everything. I think we have done pretty well, considering."

"Yes, I suppose so, but it rather takes the conceit out of a fellow to meet with so many obstacles. Why, I always thought I was good in making my way through tangled woods, but I begin to think that I am not."

"There is one thing you have forgotten, Jack. We are in the tropics, the woods here are regular jungles and the temperature is something considerably above what you have been used to. You must not scold yourself too much, Jack. I think we have done very well—'sh, what's that!" in a hoarse whisper, and looking around him with alarm.

"Some one coming, Dick. Hide, quick!"

CHAPTER XVIII

IN THE LAIR OF THE FOX

The boys quickly secreted themselves in the high grass, and in a few moments several men came into the glade, evidently in great excitement.

"We've got to get him quick," said one. "Is this the right way, do you think? We can't waste no time waiting around here with that revenue cutter hanging around."

"Him and Davis went over to this side 'cause he wanted to show Davis that there was a vessel in the bay, and now this here other one is hanging about, and she may come to our side and find us," said another. "This here is the way, I think, but I ain't sure."

"Well, come on and find him," growled a third man. "As you say, we'd better not waste no time with a revenue cutter hanging about and looking for us. Come on!"

The men hurried on, and when there was no longer any sign of them Jack arose and said:

"They have seen a vessel outside, probably from one of the hills, and have taken the alarm. It is likely that this is the vessel Mr. Smith has sent to get us out. I hardly believe she is a revenue cutter, although these men would hardly be deceived on that point."

"They might," said Percival. "They would take alarm at anything. I think myself that it is likely to be the vessel sent to get us out. She should be here by this time, according to our calculations. Let us get on the hill, Jack, and have a look at her ourselves. We may be able to tell what she is if we can get a good look at her."

"Very good," and the boys at once struck out in a direction which they judged would take them into one of the paths leading to the northern end of the island.

They reached one in five minutes, and then pushed on till they came to the open, and in another few minutes came out upon a higher level whence a fairly good view of the open sea could be obtained.

"There she is!" cried Jack, pointing out to sea. "She is a cutter, Dick. The men were right. She is under a good head of steam, too, as you can tell by the smoke pouring from her funnels. She is cruising about here, and is evidently in search of some one. Perhaps she suspects that Davis is in here, and is trying to locate him."

The boys watched the cutter for ten minutes, and then saw her alter her course, and take one which would bring her around to the other side of the island.

"I wonder if Storms has seen her?" said Jack. "I don't believe she knows the way in here. If she did she would have come in. She is going away. We won't see her in a short time."

"I don't wonder that the smugglers were alarmed. Well, if she goes to the other side Rollins may leave unless he is hidden in a cove, the same as Davis is. The latter will have a good chance to get out if the coast is clear. She is getting farther and farther off, Jack."

"Yes, and we won't see her in a little while. She is probably going to the other side to look for these fellows. Well, we have not seen exactly what we came out to see, but we have seen something, and I think we had better go back. It is getting later than I thought."

The boys, accordingly, set off toward the shore, and at length reached it, finding Ben Bowline waiting for them with the boat.

"Your Flying Dutchman was a real vessel, Ben," said Jack, "and she is hiding in a cove along shore, but just where I can't tell you. I would have to look for her. Did you see the revenue cutter outside?"

"No, we did not. Revenue cutter, hey? Not the vessel that's coming to take us out, sir?"

"No, but a revenue cutter. She is looking for your Flying Dutchman, I imagine, or for another smuggler. This place seems to be a favorite hiding place for such craft."

"Well, they're welcome to it, sir, for if we get out all right they can have it to themselves, for all o' me."

"The trouble is how to get out, Ben," said Percival. "Whichever way you turn there seems to be some difficulty ahead of you."

"Yes, and that reminds me of a time when I was sailing around the coast of Africky lookin' for slavers. Ever heard tell about it!"

"No, but you must be older than I thought, Ben, to have been alive at that time. There have been no slavers for sixty years or more around these parts, and you wouldn't— —"

"Well, there was slavers for all that," persisted Ben. "I didn't say I was chasin' American slavers. They is others, or was. Portuguese an' other fellows was in the business in them days. Well, anyhow, talking about meetin' trouble wherever you turn, this here adventure o' mine was that sort."

"What was it, Ben? We have time to listen to it before having to start back, I guess, or you can tell it to us while you are rowing us out to the yacht."

"Well, we was cruisin' around the Guinea coast, and one day I went on shore to look about and got separated from the other fellows, and all to once got so tangled up in the jungle that I didn't know which way to go nor nothing."

"That's interesting," said Percival.

"Then all of a sudden about forty black niggers jumped out of the jungle and gave chase, for I didn't stop to calc'late which way I orter go when I seed them, but just laid a course what would take me away from 'em the quickest.

"I just put through the jungle as tight as I could jump, and suddenly come face to face with a scrouching lion as big as a elephant, all ready to pounce upon me, and there I was between two fires.

"You might say three, because I was on the edge of a swamp and there was a big alligator with his mouth wide open, ready to swaller me the minute I got into the swamp."

Percival gave Jack a knowing wink and said:

"Well, that was a dilemma. What did you do?"

"Well, I just didn't know what to do, 'cause whichever way I went there was danger. The lion and the 'gator was in front an' the savage niggers behind, and it was as bad to stand still as to run and no port in a storm."

"Well?" and Dick gave Jack a wink.

"I just didn't do nothin', 'cause good luck did it for me. The niggers run plump into the jaws of the lion or smack into the 'gator, an' in a brace o' shakes one an' t'other was so stuffed full o' meat that they had no appetite for me, an' I just laid a course down the river an' found my mates in a jiffy."

"That's another steal from Baron Munchausen with a few variations," laughed Percival. "Did you ever hear of him, Ben?"

"Huh! they's no 'arthly use o' spinin' any yarns to you, young gentlemen, 'cause you don't believe 'em nohow," muttered Ben in a disgusted tone, and then he gave way upon the oars and did not say another word.

When the boys reached the vessel, shortly before dinner, Jack told the captain of what he had heard and seen, the officer being greatly interested, and saying shortly:

"If the fellow in the cove has a pilot on board maybe we can hire him to take us out or maybe force him to do it. You couldn't signal to the cutter, I suppose?"

"No, we had no means. She has gone to the other side of the island now, probably in search of the other vessel. You have not had any message from the one that is coming to our assistance?"

"No, I have not, but I expect her to-day or to-morrow. Could you find the cove where the smuggler is hidden?"

"I might," answered Jack thoughtfully.

"If I can find her before she gets out," the captain continued, "I'll catch him, and make him take us out of the bay to the open. Then I'll turn him over to the cutter, and get the reward. These fellows captured one of our vessels, and it'll be only turn about, which is fair play for everybody."

"Are your men armed?" asked Jack. "Remember, these men are ready for fight at any moment. They always expect it, and are prepared. They act in defiance of the government, and know that if caught they will be imprisoned, and they are always on the defensive."

"Yes, I know that, but if I can take them by surprise they won't have a chance to fight."

"Well, I will try to find the cove for you, sir, but, of course, I cannot join in any fight you may have with the smugglers. The doctor would not allow it."

"No, I suppose not, and quite right, too. I'll see that you don't get into trouble on our account, but I do want to catch this chap, and make him take us out of here."

"I heartily hope that you will, Captain," said Jack.

After dinner the yacht steamed out into the open bay, inside the reefs, and a lookout was kept for the cutter, which might still be in the neighborhood, and at the same time Captain Storms told the doctor what he had contemplated, and asked his permission to take Jack as a pilot to discover the whereabouts of the smuggler.

"He will be in no danger, I trust?" asked Dr. Wise, glaring at the captain, as was his wont when greatly interested.

"I will look out for that, sir," replied the captain. "He and his chum were looking for this fellow this morning, and found out where he lay, from the shore. I think he will be able to locate him from the water, and if he does I'll have the rat out of his hole in a brace of shakes, provided you will let me have him."

"Why, yes, I think so," rejoined the doctor, looking as wise as his name would indicate. "I am most anxious to get away from here, and if you think there is a chance of it I am quite willing to let you use your own judgment. You know best about such matters."

A boat was lowered containing the captain, Jack Sheldon, Dick Percival and six stout sailors, the entire party with the exception of the boys, being heavily armed.

A second boat, in charge of the mate, was lowered, and followed the first at a little distance, the officer having orders to close up quickly in case it became necessary.

Jack sat in the stern with the captain, and, as they skirted the shore, kept a sharp lookout for any possible inlet to the cove where the smuggler lay in hiding.

There was a full tide, and this enabled them to go closer to the rocks than if it had been low, and Jack peered into every opening in the hope of finding the right one at last.

At length as they were proceeding slowly at a safe distance from an ugly looking mass of rocks, which projected to some distance into the water, and where there were dangerous looking eddies, Jack noticed a steeple shaped rock higher than the rest, and at some little distance in shore.

"That is the rock I could not get around, Dick," he said to Percival. "Of course, I cannot from here see the rock from which I looked down on the men in the boat, but I know that rock well. Keep on, Captain, and watch. I think I can find the way now."

"There was a turn in the passage, wasn't there, Jack?" asked Dick.

"Yes, but there may have been others, and I think that the general direction of the inlet was about east. I shall look for it at any rate."

They kept on slowly, Jack directing them closer in to shore, and looking sharply for any sign of the channel, which he presently detected by keeping his eye on the water.

At a point where the rocks seemed to have no opening he detected a motion toward the bay, and, knowing that the tide was now on the ebb, had the captain steer closer in to the rocks.

"You won't run us onto them, sir?" whispered Storms.

"No, sir. Look toward them. Can't you see that the tide is setting this way, that there is no eddy, but the regular flow of the tide?"

"By gravy! yes, I do," exclaimed the captain hoarsely. "Keep on, my boy, and I believe you'll find the place."

Jack watched the water, steered in closer, and suddenly, in rounding a blunt point, saw the entrance to the cove before him, and noticed that the tide was running steadily out of it toward the sea.

"Here we are, sir," he said to the captain, and at once the other boat was signaled, and came up in a few moments.

Both proceeded up the creek side by side, and at length Jack saw the rock whence he had watched the men in the boat, and pointed it out to Percival, together with the one like a steeple, which had first called his attention to the place.

There was room for the two boats abreast, the passage being wide enough for a good-sized vessel to pass, and they kept on side by side, past the bend in the inlet, and then on and around another, suddenly coming in sight of a vessel at anchor.

"That's the *Circe*, the steamer that was taken by the smugglers," said the captain. "I know her well, though I never sailed in her. They've painted out her name, but that's her, I'll take my oath."

At a signal from the captain the two boats dashed forward, and were alongside the steamer before any one on board knew of their approach.

The captain and mate, followed by four men from each boat, scrambled up the side like monkeys, and made a dash for the cabin as a man came out and demanded gruffly:

"Hello! who are you, and what do you want?"

"That's Davis," said Jack. "I know his voice. We have made no mistake."

"Of course not," said Percival "Do you see that fender hanging over the side? These fellows have forgotten it. There is your name *Circe*, as plain as you please."

"Yes, I see it."

"There are lively times up there, Jack," Dick continued. "I'd like to join in it."

"Let the men go instead," laughed Jack. "We can look after the boats."

"All right. Up with you, men!" and the invitation was accepted in a moment.

CHAPTER XIX

THE WAY OUT FOUND

The men scrambled out of the boats and on deck as soon as they had the boys' permission, and for a minute or two there was the liveliest sort of fracas on the deck and in the cabin of the *Circe*, but this shortly ceased, and the mate coming to the side leaned over and said:

"We've got 'em! They put up a fight, but everything is dead against them. This is our company's vessel, and we've found enough unstamped stuff in the cabin to give 'em a good long rest in jail. We've got Davis, the captain, but the other fellow is over on the other shore, unless he has made his escape by this time. Come on board, boys."

The boys quickly accepted the invitation, and went on board where they found Davis and his men prisoners.

There was not a large crew, and some of them had been asleep at the time of the surprise, these being captured before they knew what was going on.

"Go aboard with the boys and all the men you need," said the captain to the mate. "I am going with the pilot. Follow us and do exactly as we do. I've got this fellow under my thumb. He knows he'll get a good long term for smuggling, but I can get some of it taken off if he pilots us out, and I've promised him to do my best for him. It'll be as hard as finding a needle in a haystack to get a pilot and we have him, so what's the use of looking?"

"Quite right, sir."

The captain stood in the pilot house with a pistol at the head of the pilot, and told him to give his orders, and to give wrong ones at his peril.

"If you sink us you'll sink yourself," he added, "so mind your chart and steer straight."

"All right, Captain," said the other. "I'll do as you say. I am not over fond of Davis, who has done me many a dirty turn, and as for Rollins, there is no more trusting him than there is a wolf, and I shall be glad to be shut of both of them and the business at the same time."

The boats were sent back to the yacht, which was put in charge of the first officer, and followed in the wake of the *Circe*.

In this case she proved to be worthier of trust than her beautiful namesake of the days of Ulysses, and she not only made her way safely out through the tortuous channel among the reefs, but led the yacht with the boys on board to the open water outside.

More than once as Captain Storms saw the waters bubbling and boiling around them, and saw how close they were to the rocks he thought that they were doomed, but as he watched the face of the pilot he saw that the man was to be trusted, and held his peace.

When they were outside, and a great cheer went up from the Hilltop boys, they proceeded to the end of the island in search of the cutter and at last saw her smoke in the distance.

Sending her a wireless message they at length had the satisfaction of seeing her approach, and at last the captain came on board and the *Circe* and her crew were turned over to him, Storms saying:

"Look out for the pilot. He is not as bad as the rest, and deserves some consideration on account of getting us out of a bad scrape. Have you caught Rollins?"

"No, he was too quick for us, and slipped away, but we'll catch him yet."

"I doubt if you do. However, never mind that. I'll put you in charge here and will go back to my own vessel."

He had been back in his own cabin but a short time, receiving the congratulations of the doctor and the boys when the man on the lookout reported a vessel in the offing, which flew the company's flag, and seemed to be familiar to many of the officers and men.

"That's the ship that Smith has sent to get us out," laughed Storms, "and we've got ahead of him, and got out ourselves."

He was correct, for in half an hour the newcomer was alongside and in a moment Mr. Smith himself was over the side and grasping his son, Jesse W., in his arms.

"But how is this?" he asked. "I thought you could not get out. Did you do this for a joke so that you could see me?"

"No, indeed, sir," said young Smith. "We have not been away from the island more than an hour or two, and it is to Jack Sheldon that you owe your getting out. Come here, Jack, I want to introduce you to my father."

"I am pleased to see you, sir," said Jack, coming up. "I am afraid that Jesse W. gives me too much credit, although I am willing to take a little of it. Captain Storms deserves the greater part of it, however."

Mr. Smith held a consultation with the captain of the revenue cutter, and an arrangement was shortly made between them whereby the *Circe* was to be in the government's custody for a time, and then to be turned over to her owners.

The whole story was told and Jack, Dick, and many of the boys came in for their meed of praise from Mr. Smith, as well as from Dr. Wise and the captain.

Mr. Smith had not found a pilot who could take him through the reefs to Lost Island, as they all still called it, but his chagrin was greatly tempered by seeing his son and all the boys safe out of their island prison, and he complimented Jack on all that he had done, and said:

"My dear boy, I have already promised my son to look after your interests, and you need have no fear that they will be thoroughly attended to."

"I am much obliged to you, sir," replied Jack, blushing, "but I am glad to have found such good friends. I want to say a few words in behalf of your son, and am only expressing the sentiments of the majority of the boys when I tell you that he is a plucky little chap, and a credit to the Hilltop Academy. I trust that we may long have him with us."

"Hurrah for Jesse W., boys, give him a rouser!" cried Percival, and they were given with a will.

Mr. Smith went back to the relief vessel, the cutter took away her prize, and by night the vessels had all parted company, Jesse W. Smith's father to return to New York, and the yacht to proceed on her cruise, which, although somewhat shortened as to route, was to continue until the time originally set as to its duration.

The cruise was a most pleasant one, and the boys learned much while it lasted, and were sorry when it ended, and they set out for the north and the Academy in the highlands.

Later the *Circe* was turned over to its owners, and a share of the reward for its recovery put to Jack's account in the bank, much to his surprise, as well as satisfaction.

The man with the white mustache, who was one of the boldest of the smugglers, had made his escape, whither he had gone no one could tell, but Jack's only interest in the man was to hope that he would keep away on account of his mother, to whom he related nothing concerning his meetings with the man, either at the Academy or in the tropics.

"I do not wish her to think of him," he said to Percival, "and I do not wish to think of him myself. Never mention him, Dick."

"You may be sure I won't!" replied Dick with emphasis.

There were some of the boys who did not escape seasickness on the way back, for all they had been on the water so long, but the run home was, on the whole, most pleasant, and Jack, Dick, young Smith and some others enjoyed it thoroughly.

"We shall have enough to think of and to talk about for a long time," remarked Jack to Percival when they were at last on the train going back to the Highlands, "and it is all the better that the trip was not what it was originally planned to be. The very unexpectedness of our adventures gave them all the greater charm."

"I suppose so," said Dick, "but I generally like to know what is coming, and then if I don't like it, I can get out of the way."

"Well, we are all of us richer in experience."

"And you in pocket," laughed Dick. "Don't forget that, my boy."

"Oh, I have something that is worth a good deal more than the money that I happened to get," said Jack, smiling.

"What is that?" asked Percival.

"The friendship of a lot of good fellows, and of one or two who are a good deal more than mere good fellows, real friends, in fact."

"Well, that is worth a good deal, of course, but it seems to me that one always has plenty of friends if he has money."

"If he keeps them when he has no money, then they are friends, indeed," said Jack, "and I think that I can count upon mine in any case."

"Then you are lucky, Jack."

For all that they had enjoyed themselves while afloat, the Hilltop boys were glad to be back at the Academy again among the old familiar scenes, and the work of the school went on with renewed vigor, Jack, in particular, giving his entire attention to it so as to be as high as possible in his classes at the end of the term.

The greater part of the boys at the Academy, as well as the doctor and all of the professors, were his friends, and the fact that some of the boys were not, and did all they could to injure him did not worry him, for he thought little or nothing of it.

At the end of the term he was at the head of his class, and was so close upon Percival that the latter said with a good-natured grin:

"You'll be up with me next term, Jack, whether I look out for myself or not."

"Well, we generally have pretty good times together, Dick," Jack replied, "so I don't think you will be sorry."

"Not a bit of it," said Dick.

Those who have been interested in following the fortunes of the Hilltop boys may be glad to continue their acquaintance with Jack Sheldon and his friends and enemies in the next volume, "The Hilltop Boys on the River," which, in addition to giving an account of many aquatic sports, contains also a number of thrilling incidents, which serve to bring out the characters of the boys to good advantage.

It was at the end of the term, and many of the boys were preparing to go home when Percival said to Jack:

"The doctor is going to let us have a summer camp for a few weeks. We are to live on the river, and have all the fun we want with the addition of some study, just to keep our hands in. What do you say, Jack? Will you stay over if I do?"

"I may stay in any event, Dick. I want to get on as fast as I can, and this will give me a chance."

"Then if you stay, so will I," heartily, "and between you and me you will find a lot more who will do it if they know you are to be here."

"The more the merrier," said Jack.

THE END

CPSIA information can be obtained
at www.ICGtesting.com
Printed in the USA
BVHW071603270519
549345BV00005B/690/P